MAYA

Manjiri Gokhale Joshi

Maya

First published in India in 2016 by Vishwakarma Publications
© **Manjiri Gokhale Joshi**
ISBN 978-93-85665-20-2
Edition - First edition October 2016

All rights reserved
No part of this publications may be reproduced, transmitted, or stored in a retrieval system, in any form or by any means, electronic, mechanical photocopying, recording or otherwise, without the prior permission of the publisher.

This is a work of fiction, Names, characters, places and incidents are either the product of the author's imagination or are used fictitiously and any resemblance to any actual person, living or dead, events or locales is entirely coincidental.

Published by:
Vishwakarma Publications 283, Budhawar Peth, Near City Post, Pune- 411 002. Phone No: (020) 20261157

Email: info@vpindia.co.in Website: www.vpindia.co.in
Cover photo: Sudheer Barve
Cover design: Meghnad Deodhar
Model: Dipali Vedak
Typeset and Layout: Gold Fish Graphics, Pune.
Printed at Repro India Ltd, Mumbai

Rs. 195/-

This book is sold subjects to the condition that it shall not, by way of trade or otherwise, be lent, resold, hired out, or otherwise circulated, without the publisher's prior consent, in any form of binding or cover other than that in which it is published.

Dedication

To the unconditional love of a generation of inspirational senior women in my family…

Dr. Vidya Gokhale, Sandhya Kalghatgi, Sudha Gokhale, Leela Phatak, Suman Joag, Vijaya Gokhale, Tara Kher, the late Ratna Bembalkar, Anuradha Bhatavdekar, Kunda Vartak, Sudha Kanitkar and Sheila Syratt

As well as

Poornima Sathe

CONTENTS

Acknowledgement vii

Foreword ix

1. Wallflower 01
2. Working woman 05
3. Outperformer 08
4. Sacrifice 11
5. Birthday bash 15
6. Carnations and above 25
7. Superwoman 32
8. Poor relations 34
9. Change of fortune 38
10. Death of a superwoman 41
11. CEO material 44
12. Green-the colour of pain 51
13. Encounter 54
14. Letting go 58
15. The closest to home 64
16. Just like the movies 66
17. Beauty and the beholder 71

18	Priorities	73
19	Supermum	81
20	Making peace	84
21	Silence	88
22	Corporate healing	91
23	Mrs. No-one	94
24	Diwali	98
25	Candle and moth	105
26	Happy birthday Urja	110
27	Abyss	114
28	Be practical	117
29	Water	121
30	Life	125
31	The power of M	131
32	Afterlife	134
33	Epilogue	143

Acknowledgements

The author wishes to thank the following for their contribution to the 'Maya' endeavour.

Abhay Joshi
Anagha Salgarkar
Aditi Akkalkotkar
Anand Thakkar
Anil Jethra
Carrol Desouza
Dipali Vedak
Gauri Gokhale
Gauri Patule
Geetha Morla
Gunjan Narula
Harsh Jethra
Hiren Jethra
Dr. Jabbar Patel
Jay Tahasildar
Kumuda Morla
Kishore Karandikar
Madan Gokhale
Mahi Joshi
Manasi Barve
Manish Kabra
Manjula Rao
Meghnad Deodhar
Neeraja Sathe
Pinky Batha
Poonam Sathe
Prajakti Nayak
Pramoda Morla

Pratyusha Lakkapragada
Ragini Jethra
Rajas Barve
G. Rajaraman
Ram Morla
Renuka Reuben
Sampada Kabra
Sangeeta Jethra
Santosh Salgarkar
Scharada Dubey
Seema Sinha
Shabana Azmi
Shamin Tahasildar
Sohum Salgarkar
Sharvari Joshi
Sonali Tahasildar
Stanley Gabriel
Sudheer Barve
Dr. Sulabha Karandikar
Dr. Suresh Gokhale
Tanvi Joshi
P. T. Usha
Trupti Chimbaikar
Dr. Vidya Gokhale
Vishal Soni
Vengalil Sreeninivasan
Vivek Giridhari

Foreword

India lives in several centuries simultaneously and her people at given time and place encapsulate all the contradictions that come from being a multi-cultural, multi religious, multi caste society, especially with regard to women.

An all-women crew operates the world's longest continuous flight, women scientists play a pivotal role in a country's Mars mission and girls continue to top school and University board exams. From the same geography emerge horrific tales of growing crime against women and inconvenient issues like domestic violence and marital rape are ROUTINELY brushed away.

A significant number of women in patriarchal societies do not have a choice – either to be born, or to access nutrition, education, health, get gainful employment, build careers, have children or not. They do not participate in the decision making process. In the same world of dichotomies, a smaller number of women have the 'luxury' of choice. 'Maya' breaks new ground in questioning how genuine that choice really is. 'Maya' explores how women who do have a choice, choose to exercise theirs and what underlying threads in the complex fabric of society influence these decisions.

'Maya' traces the journey of a middle class girl who is willing to compromise at every step to achieve her goals of belonging to the upper class and having a fruitful marital relationship. As the self-indulgence of childhood gives way to awkward adolescence and a young girl steps into the role of consort, the compromise begins. As a 40-year old socialite wife of a CEO, Maya achieves both goals, until life throws a rude shock. Breaking under the weight of having gone to great lengths to further her husband's career, giving up far too much, in fact trying too hard to make things work, Maya finally finds the strength to pick up life's threads again.

Maya's journey is not unique. Her firm ideas as a middle class Indian girl on what women should and should not do-speak for society as it was in the 1980s and sadly, even in 2016 in parts of the world. We encounter Maya everyday, not just in the movies, but in real life…wives and mothers who tightly wrap their lives around the priorities set by the men in their lives.

There is a Maya in each of us who is made to believe that achievement is not an asset but a burden, who is made to suppress ambition and feel guilty about celebrating her success lest she over-shadow the man in her life! As women slip into roles of girlfriend, fiancé, wife and mother, the suppression of their own desires appears ever so natural. Is the subtle but sure pressure to downplay one's capability, the only route to a happy marriage? Is a compromise at every step really a choice? Liberation is not about shouting slogans but having the freedom to express oneself and to live life on one's own terms.

The book is a gentle reminder to the modern urban woman and man that laws and policies to a great extent have enabled gender equality-the only barrier that remains is a set of ingrained social norms and stereotypes epitomised by 'Maya' and the matchmaker's notions of what women should do. A woman exuding independence spells trouble for a man's ego. It is only when women find the courage to step out of these social confines that the journey towards genuine gender equality will truly begin.

Shabana Azmi

Shabana Azmi is one of India's finest film and theatre actresses having been conferred with the Padmashree and the Padmabhushan by the Indian Government and a glittering string of awards. A former Member of Parliament and social activist, she continues to espouse the cause of gender equality across the world.

1

WALLFLOWER

"My husband never laid a finger on me. Domestic violence? My dear, how gross!" said Maya, daintily picking at her raw papaya salad. With the ease of one used to eating, or rather be seen eating exotic food at just the right locations, needless to say, with just the right cutlery, Maya placed her fork down and dabbed off a non-existent piece of papaya from her thin lips. Even as she continued to air her views on this "gross" social problem to her chatty kitty party audience, she was pleased to note that the 'non-transfer' lipstick she picked up last week had not transferred on to the crisp white table napkin.

"Lipstick stains on glasses and napkins were gross too. Almost as gross as this subject of domestic violence," thought Maya, mentally ticking off how many of the diamond-dripping wives around her used non-transfer lipstick and how many of them had been beaten up by their husbands. Though none of these women lounging in the upscale restaurant would admit it in public, Maya knew it was not so uncommon. Even on that particular day, she could imagine one of them camouflaging an angry bruise on her forehead with layers of make-up before she made it to the kitty party.

Maya impatiently swept aside the memory of that lipstick stain on Rahul's tie she had discovered, thinking, "Hadn't the woman heard of non-transfer lipstick? It was so much like a B-grade Bollywood movie. Of course, Rahul had laughed away the notion that there could be a lipstick stain on his tie. He had brushed away Maya's silly idea merrily remarking that his company's public relations department was into big-time 'Indian welcomes' for overseas customers these days and the red mark was just a part of the paraphernalia for the ceremonial red tikas on the forehead and garlands! Maya knew he could be right but it could well be a lie. Still there was no wife-beating nonsense in Maya's life."

"All this domestic violence is so gross." said Maya shaking her head.

"Maya, Maya, what trip have you been on? They are talking about something else. No one's discussing domestic violence any more." Maya was startled out of her reverie with Preeti's discreet whispering and nudging.

Preeti Mitra, Maya's best friend and confidante. Preeti Mitra, who knew Maya years before Rahul Sikand's career sky-rocketed from his humble beginnings and Mrs. Maya Sikand latched on to Preeti's own kitty party/charity event/card session 'circuit'. Among the 15 odd immaculately dressed women at the table in the five-star restaurant, only Preeti had known Maya in her days before she could afford the opulence that the others had always taken for granted. Preeti had known Maya since the days when Maya would quietly (and she had thought discreetly) compare prices of different brands of soap, shampoo and even cooking oil and rice, and pick the cheapest, flippantly remarking that there was something about this product that others could not match.

Even during those days and even when Preeti realized that Maya was just trying to make the most of the joint income Rahul and she managed to bring in every month, Preeti never commented. Given her own illustrious background, Preeti had never ever had to check price tags before she piled up a shopping cart, but Preeti understood Maya and was never judgmental about what her closest friend did. Even as Rahul puffed and stretched himself to reach the pinnacle of professional success, Maya had worked hard too, on their social image. With Preeti as a willing and yet, unassuming crutch and largely due to her own skills at opportunistic social climbing, Maya shattered the glass ceiling and emerged, unscathed into the 'elite wives' circuit.

The gentle clink of expensive crockery, the liveried service and the easy flow of money around her was proof that she had truly arrived. Money- there was lots of that on the table at that very moment. The dessert dishes cleared as they waited for coffee, the wives had opened their little handbags, stuffed primarily with toiletries and credit cards. There were 15 of them and the monthly contribution was Rs. 10,000/- per head. What would the lucky one for that month do with the kitty? Pick up a new pair of diamond earrings? More clothes, more jewellery, more accessories, more little handbags, more sleek shoes?

"The latest model of the diamond-encrusted cell phone handset would be cool. The bulky ones look quite gross. They didn't even fit into the little handbag-once the basic make-up kit and wallet was in." thought Maya. She also thought it was gross to be seen with a paper diary. She decided that the kitty amount would be best utilized on that absolutely charming "women's hand phone". Maya could just imagine Charu Batra turning green with envy the next time Maya's hand phone rang in public.

Charu, the fat head who could barely manage to use her cell phone, who would never figure out text messaging or worse, who was completely ignorant of the fact that cell phones could be set on silent mode! Be it the hippest fashion show in town or a formal condolence gathering, Charu's cell phone would ring and ring, in loud, shrill tones, and Charu would fumble, first to fish it out of her over-stuffed handbag and then even longer, to answer it. And then in a hoarse whisper, "Hello ji Mrs. Batra this side! Kaun ji, haanji, jaroor ji, call back karungi aapko vaapas." (Who is this? I will call back again). Charu, the fat head would fumble again to disconnect.

"Gross! These mannerisms of Charu, the fat head were so gross!" thought Maya, wondering why she even bothered to put up with her. But unfortunately

Maya

for Maya, the fat head's social standing or more important, her husband's monetary value was fatter than most of the 15 women around that table. So all of them tolerated her. Maybe the same reason why they included Maya in their fold too. Besides, Maya had tried hard enough to 'belong'. She had been trying it for longer than she could remember.

And this was just one of the several kitties Preeti and Maya were part of. Even as Maya briskly placed her own bundle of 10 crisp red Rs. 1000 notes on the table, the irony hit her. It was very rare that Maya's mind flashed back to the days when things were not all that good. But today, as she lay down that Rs. 10,000/- bundle, Maya's mind flashed to the days, not all that long ago, when her monthly salary cheque would read a little over half that amount after an entire month of 10- hour workdays.

2

WORKING WOMAN

Years of indulgence had given Maya the sophisticated moneyed look that she had always yearned for in her mother when she attended parent-teacher interactions in school. Maya's mother – Sunayana, despite her sober taste in cotton saris, had a distinct "working woman" look. Sunayana's sari was always neatly pinned across her left shoulder. She always lugged around a largish handbag stuffed with papers, errand books, laundry bills, grocery lists, ration card, sunglasses, comb, safety pins and other such paraphernalia. During Maya's own "working woman" years, she had struggled to not acquire that "Sunayana-like working woman persona."

Maya thought of the ten-hour workdays when a filthy, smelly, over-crowded Delhi Transport Corporation (DTC) bus would deposit her at the bus stop at Connaught Place. Another 10 minute walk, battling the city's sweltering summer or freezing winter and Maya would be at her office, a place she hated. She wondered what she had hated more: the drudgery of those dusty files in that lawyer's office, the pittance her efforts fetched her, or the mad scramble back home to get dinner in order after yet another long day at the office.

Actually, it was none of these that Maya detested. For Maya was far from lazy. Though her work as an assistant to a lawyer did not inspire her, she was sincere and meticulous with the tasks assigned to her. If asked to rate her as an employee, her boss would have described her as dependable and professional.

The first adjective would have come from the fact that Maya never shirked work, despite the not-so-evident fact that she endured her workplace and the people in it, solely because she needed the money. The adjective "professional" came from the fact that Maya would never be caught gossiping. Unlike the women (and men) who thrived on chunks of information on the boss' personal life, tid-bits on the philandering of other employees and the like, Maya had no interest whatsoever in the lives of her co-workers. These people had made the law firm the centre of their lives. They were here to stay. Most of them, she knew, would either hop on to other law firms with similar job profiles or else retire with "best compliments" and a wall-clock, from the same firm at the ripe old age of 60.

Maya harboured an arrogant dislike of both options. She knew she would leave, chuck those files and run, as soon as she got a higher paying job or when (not if, Maya was certain) Rahul hit the jackpot and did not need his wife to chip in with the household expenses, whichever came earlier.

As for the boss, the senior lawyer himself, far from being fascinated like her colleagues, Maya was not even curious about the fancy lifestyle he supposedly led. Maya in fact, found him "decidedly middle class pushed into upper middle class and unable to carry off his new found status." The assessment, though accurate, had a certain sense of irony, coming as it did from Maya, who had known no other lifestyle except the "decidedly lower middle class one" that her parents had offered her.

But the reason Maya hated all of these, as well as her work, was far different. Maya hated the "working woman" tag. Unlike thousands of women across the world, who straddled the dual demands of work and home for what they thought gave them "financial independence, intellectual growth, and mental satisfaction" Maya never wanted to work in an office. Of course, now she thought it was "gross" to be handed a salary by some middle-class accountant in an office, a pittance that would not even cover her restaurant bills for a week. But even back then, when she and Rahul really needed the Rs. 6000/- she brought in every month, she'd squirm at being viewed as a "working woman".

For Maya, the term "working woman" denoted the things she despised:

1) Is short of money i.e. the man does not earn enough, so the wife needs to chip in.

2) Belongs to the middle or upper middle class. In Maya's perception of the world, upper class women did not work for anyone else. They either ran companies inherited from their fathers or occupied themselves with boutiques or art galleries their husbands set up for them.

3) Competes with her husband. It signified a thirst for equality and sense of competition in the man-woman relationship that she had tried to escape from, all her life.

Maya's strategy in avoiding this "equality equation" was to underplay her ability. She had been doing it ever since she met Rahul. If Rahul said something inaccurate, and Maya knew better (she often did though she would not admit it), she would never, ever correct him.

For donkey's years, matchmakers had written the rule books: A short groom needed a bride shorter than him and a man with limited means ought to have a wife from a poor family so that she'd "adjust better." When the "arranged marriage" tradition carried over well into an age when urban Indian society had sprouted egalitarian wings, the match-maker's mantras reigned supreme: "A woman should never earn more than her husband, so that there is peace in the marital home. And to ensure that the woman does not earn more than her husband, she should be less qualified." Maya was the very embodiment of these principles and followed them to the hilt.

3

OUTPERFORMER

In spite of Maya's obsession with the lower, middle and upper class divide and her notions of what one class of people did and did not do, Maya knew that domestic violence knew no such barriers. The fact that women from all strata of society preferred to endure domestic violence in order to remain married, further strengthened her belief that a woman exuding independence and efficiency spelt sure trouble to a man's ego.

She thought of the sob-story that her domestic help related to her – a drunken husband smashing her glass bangles, brutally banging her against the wall, all for that extra Rs. 100/- note hidden inside her sari blouse. For the husband, that thin, mousy looking mill-worker, the violence was a form of release and a balm for his own brutally bruised ego. For Ram Sharan, the victim of the sackings that followed the mill-strike, it was a symbol of the circumstances that made Neelam Kali, his wife of 8 years, superior to him. Neelam Kali, the village nymphet he had wedded when she was barely 15 years old; the girl who had timidly followed him on the train from the nondescript village in Bengal to the fascinating city of Dilli.

At a speed which Neelam herself could not fathom, the nymphet had been forced to shed her veil, her near blind admiration for her "city returned" husband and more important, the lost, innocent look in her dark, doe-like eyes. The loose end of her sari no more over her dark oiled hair, Neelam learnt to deftly wind it around her waist and tuck it firmly into the petticoat. The Mems and Sahibs in Dilli had little patience for "untrained" village women like Neelam. She soon discovered that the sari-tucked look and the defiance she acquired after changing jobs as a domestic help in quick succession earned her a better salary. Her halting Hindi, (gleaned mainly from the Hindi movies they watched on TV back home in her village in West Bengal), gradually gave way to a smattering of "haanji-bibiji" peppered Dilli lingo, amply garnished with English for the Mem's benefit, all delivered in her Bangla drawl. Neelam also displayed an enterprising spirit that Ram Sharan had never imagined her to be capable of. Soon after there were signs of a new family moving into the up market locality (at the edge of which they and other migrants had taken up little huts), Neelam would be the first of the maids to swoop down onto the Mem's front door. Even as a harried young woman or man opened the door into a drawing room full of unpacked boxes and suitcases, Neelam would launch her spiel.

The knowledge of the area (where Neelam would say she'd pick up fresh vegetables, milk, bread and eggs for the family from) would help. So would her skill at customizing her appeal to suit humans of different temperaments, needs and upbringing. If the woman in question wore *sindoor* and bangles, or if Neelam sensed the presence of an older generation in the house, (an older woman-most likely, the Mem's mother-in-law) lurking in the background, Neelam would launch into an unstoppable monologue to prove her Hindu credentials.

"Ammi Bengali, West Bengal, full Indian." she would blurt out, rolling three languages into a sturdy crutch to prove that she had no links with the minority community in India and nor was she an illegal immigrant from Bangladesh. Nobody had ever told her and such insight was certainly not part of the "lessons in urban life" that Ram Sharan had given her for the first few days after they arrived in New Delhi. But Neelam had quickly gathered that some Hindus, even in urban India, however secular and "religious roots free" they might appear otherwise, were uncomfortable handing over their kitchens to a maid from the minority community. And this was particularly true of the older generation and the conservative among the younger lot.

Displaying the same sharpness, Neelam would alter her personality to appear "suitable" to work for homemakers or working women. Among the first few subtle queries she would make, Neelam would grasp the working/stay-at-home status of the woman of the house. To a typical homemaker, Neelam would say she'd chop the vegetables, knead the dough and "learn from Bibiji how her family would like *Bibiji's* own style of cooking." Neelam would smartly leave out adjectives that indicated control over the kitchen.

On the other hand, if *Bibiji* happened to be a jet-setting Madam who zipped in and out of her home at a pace that matched or was faster than her husband's, Neelam would play the classic fairy Godmother to blow away all the domestic worries of 'today's woman of substance.' Neelam would confidently convey that not only could she cook very well (and dish up calorie-free meals if Madam wanted them so), but she could also plan menus, shop for them in advance and even serve sahib and feed the kids if Madam got delayed at work. Even as she observed the smiles of relief lighting up Madam's harassed face, Neelam knew that such language and concepts of any direct communication between the maid and the man of the house were strictly taboo in stay-at-home Bibiji's domain.

The bottom line— Neelam Kali had slipped beautifully into the life and role of a standard New Delhi's most-wanted, trained and thus highly paid domestic helper. And for this success story and for all the failures that the combined forces of bad luck, fatalistic attitude, inertia, and a brooding constitution offered Ram Sharan, he beat her up, almost every night.

Maya's own mother Sunayana, had been a lawyer who outdid her husband's modest career and according to Maya, ruined all their lives in the bargain. Her views thus reinforced by scattered examples of couples she encountered in her life, Maya was determined to underplay herself in her quest to be the perfect wallflower wife.

4

SACRIFICE

When Maya met Rahul, she had been studying architecture and was considered one of the most talented and promising students in her class. Rahul was essentially a floater with big dreams awaiting enlightenment on life's calling.

With still no clue on Rahul's calling, but with the uncanny conviction that he would make it big someday, Maya decided she loved him, would most definitely marry him and would make him a wonderful, caring wife. With that supreme confidence and the conviction that a wife ought not to be better qualified than her husband in order to ensure a successful marriage, Maya chucked away her architecture course one day, just like that. Her mother had given her money to pay her second year course fees. With absolutely no regrets about chucking a career, which she as well as her teachers and classmates knew she would excel in, Maya decided she would never step into the College of Architecture ever again. Instead, she walked into the College of Arts across the street and enrolled into the Bachelor of Arts course. The Arts course fees were a fraction of the money her mother had given her and Maya promptly deposited the rest of the amount into a piggy bank entitled "encouraging and investing in Rahul's dreams." Just like that.

Maya had not bothered with announcing this decision at home. She had simply stopped attending architecture classes and had started attending Arts College. When Maya's mother finally found out, she was livid. But Maya honestly did not care.

After the highly demanding architecture curriculum, Maya found herself with a lot more time on her hands. Meeting Rahul took up most of it, but she also found herself drifting into the company of a new bunch of friends. Maya was the "new girl" in class and she quickly endeared herself to an elitist all-girls group. Mitali, the daughter of one of Delhi's most influential political figures, Sneha, who had a diamond merchant for a father, and Siya, whose parents owned one of Delhi's most successful chain of furniture showrooms. When Maya started "hanging out" with these three, they had little idea about her financial and social background. Maya had mentioned in passing that her mother was a lawyer and her father a banker. The latter was but a slight twist of terms and the impression it conveyed. Maya did not see why her father could not be described as a banker. He did work in a bank, didn't he? Maya told her new friends just that. The way they saw it, Maya was always very well dressed, crisp cotton salwar kameezes, jeans and T-shirts and occasionally, knee length skirts teamed with well-cut blouses; Maya wore simple but elegant clothes.

She had a nose for discount offers and clearance sales offered by some of the best clothes shops in town and made sure she made the most of her pocket money by being at the right sale at the right time. Even better, Maya's tailor knew how to replicate chic South Extension ware at a fraction of the price. In effect, Maya could easily pass off as one of them and as long as she appeared decently outfitted, they did not mind being spotted with her. Besides, Maya's bright mind could not be hidden for too long- she made witty, interesting conversation. And more important, she came across as a warm, friendly and extremely helpful girl.

The four of them would often go out for lunch or catch a movie by bunking a class or two. The first time Maya went out for a meal with them, she was appalled at the quantity of food ordered and subsequently left behind on the table. They'd snap shut their eternally overloaded wallets having dumped a round figure usually much higher than the contribution for the meal. "I'm not hungry." Mitali would say half way through her soup. Not just the soup, but also the meal to follow, would be left unfinished. Or else, Siya would abandon her pasta after barely a few bites saying it was rather tasteless.

Maya would be itching to open her mouth and yell at them to stop wasting food. In her mind's eye, she would compare these frequent sojourns with the rare occasions that she would eat out with her family. Maya's eyes would scour the menu card for the most exotic dish (i.e. something she had not tried before). To Maya, it was not so much the consumption of the food that would matter. It was more the statement of having been to this restaurant and that. The variety of food that she constantly yearned for was not so much out of gastronomic needs as it was to appear knowledgeable about the culinary delights that these places offered. Maya's mother of course, would be extremely matter of fact about the whole eating out experience and would ultimately decide what was to be ordered. Her father, though he would never dare say it out of the fear of criticism, Maya knew, would be looking at the right side of the menu and his thought processes would go somewhat like this,

"Trust Sunayana to select an expensive restaurant like this. So what if it was their umpteenth wedding anniversary. How did it matter? But it's alright, Maya wanted to go too and Maya ought to have the best."

Maya could not help but notice that every time she or Sunayana would mention a dish to be ordered, her father's eyes would flit toward the corresponding price on the right, his accountant brain rapidly calculating what the final tally would be like. He would always make sure he would select the most inexpensive item on the list, for he also wanted to make sure he would be able to pay the entire bill. He knew Sunayana would draw immense pleasure from picking up the tab, one more time, and for the sake of his own image before his only daughter, he wanted to be able to pay.

And irrespective of who would pick up the tab, it was understood that not a morsel of extra food would be ordered or left over at the table. The bill, when it arrived, would be closely examined, the prices of individual items calculated, percentage of sales tax levied re-checked, and then only would the exact amount, along with a few extra rupees grudgingly shelled out as a tip. For any other social being brought up on such a staple diet of strong middle class values, Mitali and Siya's wastage of food would have appeared morbid.

But Maya, startled and thus appalled the first time she encountered it, took it in her stride as yet one more of the things she herself would not do, but was willing to overlook in those whose company she enjoyed. Though she would never encourage wastage of food, she rather fancied the idea of not looking at the prices on a menu card and not having to check the bill before paying up. This "adding up" was yet another "very middle class" habit that Maya now considered "gross."

The truth was that Maya abhorred all things middle class. She had yearned desperately and fought valiantly, all her life to belong to a life that she occasionally and partially had access to view.

5

BIRTHDAY BASH

Though she attended classes, crammed for exams, lunched and went out to the movies with Mitali, Siya and Sneha, they dropped her like a hot potato when the "rest of their gang" entered the picture. Blissfully unaware of these strategic equations and naively believing that she had truly been accepted, Maya once made the mistake of attending Siya's birthday bash. Maya's own birthday celebrations in recent years had been restricted to a festive lunch or dinner at home or, depending on what she wanted to convey to her current circle of friends and how much money her mother was willing to part with, Maya would have a quiet treat for her friends in a trendy, but not phenomenally expensive restaurant.

The prospect of attending a 'real party' had Maya all excited and apprehensive at the same time. A 'real party' signifying drinks, dancing, and lots of very well dressed people, meant that she had to do something about her clothes. Thankfully, her mother had no comments to offer when Maya brought home a new pair of black suede shoes. The black skirt that Rahul had bought her on her birthday would do fine and she'd got her tailor to replicate a cream colored top she'd seen on a South Extension mannequin.

Maya

The day began well enough. Maya called Siya first thing in the morning to wish her. When they met in college, she rushed across to embrace her and presented her with a bunch of pale pink roses - Siya's favorite color, she knew. After morning classes were over, giggling away at Sneha's slick cameo on the economics professor's thick South Indian accent, all of them rushed off home, Maya yelling out that she'd see them all at the party by 8 pm.

After assuring her mother several times that Mitali's chauffeur would drop her home on the dot of midnight, Maya arrived at Siya's bungalow in an auto-rickshaw. It was exactly 8 p.m. and Maya got off the three-wheeler a few houses away from her destination. Obviously she did not want to be seen alighting from this noisy contraption, decided Maya. Mitali, Sneha and Siya knew that Maya took a bus to college. But still, a party was different and it was best the other guests did not form any opinions about her on the basis of the mode of transport she had used to get there.

Equally important was the fact that an auto-rickshaw ride could ruin one's appearance. Maya needed to pat down her windblown hair, coax it into place and also touch up her lipstick before she breezed into Siya's home. Chauffeurs, she knew, were expected to pretend that rear-view mirrors did not exist, when Madam performed her toilette in the back seat. But auto-rickshaw drivers, at least the ones in New Delhi, were a breed apart and would blatantly ogle if passengers like Maya tried any of this!

Maya waited till the auto-rickshaw sputtered away, hurriedly brushed her hair, re-touched her lips and made her way to the tall iron gates of Siya's majestic bungalow. The doorman let her in, subtly noting the absence of the purr of an automobile driving away. Maya ignored him, strode right into the lobby and then straight toward the sprawling drawing room where strains of party music summoned her.

Instead of the buzz of conversation and Siya's warm welcome she had expected, Maya was shocked to see a smattering of empty chairs and tables, a bar-man tinkering with glasses and a DJ testing audio systems on the makeshift stage. Just as she was about to step back into the lobby, the DJ turned to her,

Birthday Bash

"Hi, Vivek George, better known as Viv," he grinned, his eyes twinkling. Maya was not sure if she was supposed to be inside this room at all, if no one else was, except the uniformed bartender and this Viv character. She was about to turn to look for signs of movement in the lobby when Viv offered some more un-solicited information about himself.

"I am a DJ at Smooze, the pub at the Maurya. I am off work tonight so that I can dish up my musical magic here. Besides, Siya's special. All of Sneha's friends are special, in fact," he smiled. Almost like an afterthought, but a genuine one he asked, "What's your name? What do you do?"

"I'm Maya, I study with Siya and Sneha," she replied. After that statement- "All of Sneha's friends are special," Maya felt stupid saying she was Sneha's friend too thinking, "Who the hell was this over-friendly DJ anyway?"

"Maya, oh Maya, the bright conversationalist, understated brilliance, the architect never to be... my, the lady herself!" Viv pirouetted and bowed, turning up his face at her, sporting an imploring smile.

"How do you know all this about me?" Maya faltered, knowing it had to be Siya or Sneha's doing. Even as a part of her felt good that her new friends did think and talk about her, she had this apprehension about what they really felt about her and what they had actually told this Viv. Viv, on the other hand, seemed a trifle disappointed that Sneha had not mentioned him to her at all. Just as Maya was about to attempt stepping back into the lobby yet another time, a rowdy bunch of girls and boys burst onto the scene. Most of them headed straight to the bar. As if on cue, Viv got up, "Got to go Maya, time for work!"

Maya knew none of the people from the rowdy bunch that burst into Siya's drawing room that evening. Viv put on his DJ act for them, strumming a song or two on his guitar as the tipsiest of them sang along and then let his CD changer tackle them with a string of raunchy Hindi film numbers.

With the entire bunch engrossed in each other and her new found friend busy entertaining them, Maya found herself slinking into a corner of the room. As she surveyed the slickly dressed, glossily made-up girls around her, Maya felt inadequate. She wondered where all of them had got their clothes from—slinky black sequined tops and leather finish trousers, little black dresses with spaghetti straps and brightly colored tiny skirts teamed with figure-hugging T-shirts in earth colors.

Suddenly, Maya's knee-length black skirt seemed long and old-fashioned and her dream cream top seemed to proclaim the fact that it was made of artificial silk procured from the Middle East. Worse, Maya realized with despair that the girls from the catering service, who were circulating the appetizers among the guests were wearing the same combination as Maya—cream and black.

Maya tried her best to stay away from the waitresses, starving in the process. She wondered where the birthday girl and her other two friends were and the reason why she was at this godforsaken party. Self-conscious, bored, hungry and lonely, Maya wished she had made up some excuse and not come here at all. "Is this how the elite entertained? Hired professionals kept the guests occupied while the hosts walked in after everyone else? And didn't Siya's parents want to even see who was at their daughter's birthday party? Maya was upset that her friends did not even care whether she had arrived at the party or not, but she knew she still had a lot to learn about the social mores of the world.

Her mind spun back to the days when her parents threw what they thought, were birthday bashes for their only daughter. Dad would take the day off. "In nationalized banks in India, one can do that," Maya thought wryly, "utilize the various 'privilege' and 'casual' leave options granted to you, for occasions like your child's birthday." What other daughters could have construed as parental love, Maya dismissed this "taking leave for every special occasion in Maya's life" as yet another of the "middle class" concepts she despised. Diamond merchants like Sneha's Dad or key political figures like Mitali's were certainly not dispensable resources to just be away from work for something as trivial as a child's birthday. India Inc just did not do these things!"

But despite her pre-conceived notions on the thorny issue of what the middle class should and should not do, Maya could not deny the fact that she had immensely enjoyed her birthdays as a child. Her Dad would drop her to school, dutifully carrying a packet of sweets to be distributed among her classmates. Mum would spend the morning baking and decorating the cake in the shape Maya had demanded that particular year and toil away the entire afternoon making snacks for the 15 odd kids and some of the parents who would turn up in the evening.

By the time Maya came home from school, elated with the hand-made birthday cards her friends had made for her, their drawing room would be transformed. A fresh colorful cotton printed sheet on the diwan in the corner, bright, embroidered cushion covers, buntings on the ceiling fan, balloons blowing from the windows and Dad perched on a stool finishing the cheery "Happy Birthday Maya" letters on the wall. With Sunayana's efficiency at its peak, the entire house would be spic and span, the kitchen sparkling even after a day of laborious cooking. Maya would be dressed in a fussy, frilly frock or ghagra choli (long Indian skirt, blouse and long flowing scarf), Sunayana herself in a fresh silk sari, masking her efforts of the day by the time the clock struck five.

The entire family would welcome each guest. Sunayana would make sure that each of Maya's friends was greeted by name and she would herself pile up each child's paper plate with goodies. Maya's Dad would be at the door to coax each father, mother, uncle or older brother entrusted with dropping children to birthday parties, to step in for a few minutes and at least have some cake. Dad would also be the most enthusiastic organizer of party games—passing the parcel, musical chairs (enabled by pushing away furniture against the walls of the drawing room) and even a carefully planned treasure hunt.

Even after Maya grew up and if she hadn't wanted to shut them out of her social life, her parents would have loved to organize her birthday parties for her. But Maya did not want homemade snacks and a re-decorated drawing room in their modest flat for a birthday celebration anymore, especially after she overheard what Siya's mother did for Siya that day. Siya's birthday celebrations had begun much before Maya arrived at the palatial home at 8 pm that evening. Apart from the party that Siya had wanted and got, Siya's mother had thrown in a surprise pool side picnic for her daughter's special friends. Siya's mother had got her personal assistant to call up each one of Siya's friends to invite them to be part of this surprise celebration.

Four cars were organized to pick each one of them from their homes and transport them to the family farmhouse on the outskirts of the city. At the farmhouse, they could try their hand at riding the horses that had been called in for the occasion, ride an elephant into the woods nearby for a "mock-hunt" or simply chill out in the pool. The personal assistant had instructed Mitali and Sneha to bring Siya to the farmhouse straight after college. Her two close friends readily agreed and in fact, managed to engage her in such deep conversation that Siya didn't even realize where the chauffeur was taking them. When they arrived at the farmhouse, Siya certainly was bowled over. Greeting her was a gleaming deep blue small car festooned with a bunch of carnations and a card, "To our darling elegant eighteen… Happy Birthday, love, Mum and Dad."

Needless to say, Siya was thrilled to bits. Her own car spelt independence, freedom from a chauffeur lurking in the background whenever she and her friends had something special to talk about. The car came with a diktat; "Siya was not to drive it to college as it was a good 20 kilo meters from home. She would be driven to college and back by her chauffeur as usual."

"Girls need their freedom nowadays. I thought Siya would be happy driving down by herself when she goes to the beauty parlor to get her monthly waxing done or drops in at the club close by for a swim." Siya's mother was to tell her friends at the club the next day. Diktats were diktats and Siya's "spare car for waxing" was not driven to college. In fact, Siya hardly ended up driving it, a better, more innovative and need-driven utility for the automobile being Viv and Sneha's rendezvous.

It was when the three ice maidens finally walked into the party and Sneha planted a kiss on Viv's nose in full public view that Maya first realized that

Birthday Bash

Viv and Sneha were 'seeing each other'. Viv was in the middle of one of his funniest DJ acts and Maya had firmed up her decision to walk out into the night, when Sneha, Siya and Mitali breezed into the room.

Full of beans that he was, Viv was performing a hilarious take on a prominent political figure in chaste Hindi. Catching sight of the trio, he deftly wove in an Urdu couplet, an ode if you please, to the "teen deviyan" (Three goddesses) at the party. What made it funnier was the fact that the couplet was delivered in the same politician's somber manner. The rendition ended with the suggestion that Sneha's splendor would put a coterie of beauty queens to shame and could the bard be forgiven if the icicle from the pretty maiden's gaze actually froze his nose and lips, leaving him speechless and unable to breathe!

Viv's audience was in splits and Sneha, pink with embarrassment but emboldened by the sheer audacity of his compliments and the fact that no one from the parental generation was present, tripped up to him and kissed his "frozen nose". The room broke out in good-natured catcalls and Viv, his eyes brimming over with affection, bowed and kissed Sneha's hand. After that, it was Viv's CD changer that led the party music and the duo slipped in and out of Siya's garden, enjoying the privacy that obviously was hard to come by.

Maya, having succeeded in appearing to be part of the furniture, was observing all this from a darkened corner of the room, away from the catering company girls and their cream and black uniforms. Sneha was wrapped up in Viv, Mitali had melted into the crowd and Siya was in the midst of a bunch of girls checking out her hair, highlighted blue. Maya inched closer, wanting to at least wish Siya, and tell her she had made it here before taking off from this party where she felt so much out of place.

Siya apparently had streaked her hair just last evening and the surprise dip in the pool that afternoon had ruined the effect. So, while the rest of the guests were driven straight to this party from the farmhouse, she, Sneha and Siya had driven over to the hairdresser's in her new car. Streaking it the same way was not possible at such short notice, so Siya agreed to highlight the top of her head blue instead. It did go with the turquoise blue hipster she was wearing.

Even as Siya concluded her narration of why she and her two friends had walked in at her own party a good 90 minutes late, she caught sight of Maya at the edge of the group.

"Hi Maya! When did you come in? Why don't you help yourself to a drink? So sorry we got late. By the way, have you met Tina, Meenal, Ritu… this is Maya, we study together," said Siya in one go, turning to the others in the group. Maya, the bright conversationalist was tongue-tied. She had been the first one to wish Siya that morning, so saying "Happy Birthday" again would have been stupid. Maya had saved up and bought Siya a beautiful wooden photo-frame engraved with "Let's be friends… always," even taking the trouble to get it wrapped in pale pink handmade paper, which Siya had mentioned she really liked. The gift lay in the recesses of Maya's handbag and she decided it was best not presented at all, at least not at this party. It was pretty no doubt, but she wondered what the others had got for Siya and didn't want to appear ridiculous.

Maybe she imagined it and nobody said a word, but Maya could feel the other girls sizing her up, curiously staring at her cream silk top, checking out her black skirt, which was obviously mass produced. Maya cringed and what could she say? That she had been slinking in the corner of the room, not even touching any of the food being passed around, as she didn't want to be mistaken for being one of the waitresses? That she felt bad that she was the only one (and Viv of course, who was here on work anyway) who had not been invited to the farmhouse picnic? The fact that Siya's Mum's personal assistant did not have her telephone number meant that Siya had never mentioned Maya at home. Sneha and Mitali could have still pitched in and suggested that she be invited too, but they obviously did not care or worse, did not want her on their hands.

Maya swallowed this bitter fact and was just about to mumble to Siya that she had to get home early when this plump, spectacled young man burst onto the all-girls group.

Birthday Bash

"Ladies, my my, where have all the pretty women been hiding all this while? Siya, you know what all this beauty around me does to my poor heart?" he said in mock despair. Siya laughed and waved him away. The other girls melted away as if by magic and Maya found herself facing this plump man with a weak heart alone.

"They call me Junaid. Never seen you around before," he said.

"I study with Siya, I am Maya," she said disinterested and wondering how she would get home. Mitali had not even acknowledged her presence and Maya did not want to just walk up to her and ask if she could use her car and chauffeur.

With Viv and Sneha having taken up positions somewhere in the garden, Viv's CD changer was doing most of the DJing now. There was some obscure Western music playing right now and this Junaid suddenly asked her if she would like to dance, or rather, led her to the floor right away. Little conversation, awkward footwork and unfamiliar music… the dance was over in no time. Maya unconsciously followed Junaid to the group of people he had emerged from. Maybe she would have a drink with him and his friends and then head home. But much to her shock and the reason for this rude gesture was one she had not been able to figure out even after all these years, Junaid stopped bang in the middle of their walk to the bar.

He turned to her and with a slight bow, said, "Thank you." Maya, who was so quick on the uptake otherwise, took a trifle longer to realize that the dude was telling her not to follow him to his group of friends and that their association had been for this dance alone. Maya swallowed this bitter pill too, vowing never ever to attend a party in which she knew no one.

The immediate problem facing her was how to get home. She wanted to avoid the Mitali option. Siya was quite obviously far too pre-occupied to bother about arranging for transport to get Maya home. Her new found and only friend on the premises was probably lost deep in the tresses of his Lady Love at that very moment. Maya decided she would go home the way she came, in an auto-rickshaw. A young girl alone in an auto-rickshaw at 11 pm in Delhi!

Maya

Her Mum would freak out and Maya herself knew it was a dangerous thing to do. But Maya could not endure this party any further and strode out onto the road. With her heart in her mouth, she hailed a three-wheeler passing by. Nothing untoward happened and she used the same strategy- getting off a few houses away and quietly letting herself in, so that her mother did not figure out that it was a scandalized but decent auto-rickshaw driver and not Mitali's sprawling car that deposited her daughter home that night.

Maya was too proud to ever express her displeasure at the way she had been ignored at Siya's party and despite the pain she felt, she wrapped up the whole incident as one more learning experience and tucked it away at the back of her mind.

6

CARNATIONS AND ABOVE

Maya slowly began to drift away from this circle of friends. At her mother's insistence (and more because she could use the extra pocket money), Maya took up a part-time assignment working with one of her mother's lawyer friends. Maya and the elite trio continued to attend classes together. The lunches and movies too continued but got fewer. Maya lost touch with the girls completely once they were through with college. Strangely, it was the over-friendly Viv who she bumped into rather often and the two of them went on to share a warm and affectionate friendship.

Years later, during a holiday in Goa, Maya and Rahul ran into Viv. He had migrated to Goa, ran a small nightclub and married a Swedish tourist who "fell in love with India and with him in that order" as he put it and enjoyed his bunch of three talented kids. Sun-tanned, greying but as quick on his feet as he always had been, Viv seemed content with what life had offered him. Viv invited Rahul and Maya home for breakfast.

A prettily laid out round table awaited them in Viv's kitchen, done up in bright shades of yellow and blue. Much to Maya's surprise, there was no hired help. Viv dished out fluffy stuffed omelettes simultaneously on two pans, his wife warmed up homemade pancakes in the oven. The kids seemed to know their way about too—slicing plum cake, pouring out fruit juice and giving the finishing touches to the table. Maya had thoroughly enjoyed breakfast with Viv's family, though she wondered if Rahul got bored. He didn't say so and he had sportingly agreed to come along when Viv invited them. Yet, Rahul and Viv had little in common and Viv had been Maya's friend during those years in college, not Rahul's.

Besides, his heady climb up the career path had corporatized Rahul's mind ... numbed it to such a degree that he now seemed to be comfortable only with conversation pertaining to his line of business. Despite the fact that Rahul surrounded himself with an impressive assortment of reading material and actually did manage to read a significant portion of what he brought home, Rahul had marginal interest in subjects other than his own.

Maya missed the Rahul who would actually enjoy eating delicious chaat with her at Delhi's busy Bengali Market. A long wait at a bus stop would most often be interrupted by a tall glass of sugarcane juice with grated ice and a dash of lemon juice—both Rahul and Maya would enjoy themselves immensely. It was not that Rahul did not like sugarcane juice or chaat anymore, but neither seemed available at the places they frequented now. Mineral water, canned juices and chaat at a "street food festival" at a five-star hotel maybe? This little tinge of nostalgic regret at the days gone by, in no way meant that Maya did not value their financial transformation and the radical social ascent it brought along. But Maya missed the camaraderie she and Rahul had once shared.

Maya's reverie this time was broken by a round of applause. Viv had brought out his guitar and his talented trio had just concluded a delightful rendition of the Goan classic "Galyat saakhli sonyachi, he pori konaachi?" Viv did seem happy. Maya wondered if he ever thought of Sneha. Starting with Siya's birthday party when she first met Viv and the next two years at Arts College, there were numerous occasions when she met Sneha and Viv together. The two of them were madly in love. Maya was amazed to see the otherwise reticent Sneha transformed into a master mimic under Viv's influence and training. Professors at the Arts College, film stars, politicians and even Mitali and Siya—Sneha spared no one and always had her mini audience in splits at the impersonation.

Maya had never seen the two of them arguing, even when THE SPLIT happened. Come to think of it, there was no formal 'break-up' at all. One fine day, Sneha's parents decided to get her married, to this handsome heir of an NRI (non-resident Indian) family. The family owned a global fast food chain among its other interests and the young man was in Delhi for a few days. At a five-star coffee shop, Sneha met up with her prospective husband and his much-married sister who lived in Delhi.

Dripping diamonds from Daddy's showrooms and clad in a ready-to-wear pale orange designer sharara Mom picked up for her, Sneha was done with her "informal engagement" barely a week later. The wedding was planned three months down the line, when the groom's family would be able to make it to India. Nobody bothered noting that the dates clashed with Sneha's final year University exams. Sneha was to fly out soon after anyway and there was no question of her studying any further, so how did the exams matter?

The wedding was held in Sneha's ancestral home in Udaipur. Mitali and Siya of course, were there. Mitali's choice of subjects being slightly different, she was through with her exam schedule. Siya had a paper on the very day of the wedding and she decided to give it a pass. Siya too had plans to fly out of India soon and she could always appear for that particular paper six months down the line.

Maya thought she had antagonized her mother enough by giving up the architecture course and did not even mention going for the wedding and giving her exams the slip. For once, Maya did not object to her family's "very middle class focus on academics." Maya heard all about the grand affair though—through the glossy sections of newspapers that deployed lifestyle section reporters to Udaipur to cover the event and more in detail, through Siya and Mitali. Apparently, there were no marigolds and tuberoses that Indian wedding ceremonies ordinarily sported. These flowers were found in abundance across most parts of India and brought colour to the occasion.

"In fact, there was no flower below the class of a carnation," wrote one lifestyle section newspaper reporter apparently knowledgeable on the subject of floral decoration trends in Indian weddings and the social classes that flowers seem to be divided into. Another lifestyle report spoke of the culinary spreads that highlighted each of the ceremonies and a fashion magazine actually did a six page feature on each of Sneha's outfits, the mojaris and jootis specially created by craftsmen from Rajasthan, and more important, the exquisite diamond jewellery that Sneha's Dad's employees had laboured on. Maya did miss the "event of the decade" no doubt, but she was part of the pre-nuptial celebrations that began in Delhi. Sneha had a poolside party for her friends the day before she and her family left for Udaipur. The groom was not part of this as he was in Agra paying his respects to his maternal grandfather, who was too old and fragile to travel to Udaipur for the wedding.

After nearly three years in the elite company of Mitali, Siya and Sneha, Maya knew what to expect. She arrived at the venue of the party a good hour after the designated time. She was wearing new sandals, a wrap-around skirt and a floral top over her swimsuit. There were a couple of heads bobbing in the pool when Maya arrived, some of them she knew after stray meetings with Sneha, Siya or Mitali. Having broken the ice, Maya was confident of being able to hold easy conversation with at least some of the guests. She expected some snooty vibes, but she knew she had to learn to handle them.

Nothing could faze Maya if she expected it. What she did not expect at all was to see Viv at Sneha's "wedding shower" poolside party. What was even more unexpected was to see Viv being his usual self. He had the boys in splits with some ribald joke that he insisted was far beneath the class of the lofty young women around him, flirted outrageously with Siya and Mitali and was gentle and caring with Sneha.

On several occasions that afternoon, she caught sight of Viv and Sneha holding hands, stealing a kiss under-water or simply looking at each other as if no one else existed. Maya wondered if a storm had erupted in Sneha's family. Had her powerful and filthy rich father arm-twisted her into that "informal engagement" with the green card holding Rajasthani blue blood?

Had Sneha's rather traditionally dressed mother threatened to end her life if Sneha did not heed to their wishes on the wedding front? Were Sneha and Viv planning to elope on his motorbike on the eve of the wedding day, with stars in their eyes and love in their hearts? No, none of that was happening either. Or did such things only happen in chic lit romances and mushy movies?

Maybe they did. But in Sneha's case apparently, none of this had happened. In fact, Sneha had not even told her family that Viv was much more than a friend who sang at parties for them. She had not told them anything at all. This is pretty much what happened.

The dude arrived from the US. Sneha's father accompanied her to the five star hotel, concluded a business meeting in another restaurant in the same hotel and met her in the lobby.

At the coffee shop, Sneha's prospective sister-in-law did most of the talking. She admired Sneha's diamond studs and twinkling pendant, told her how well known her family was and how her younger brother would rather meet her alone at a coffee shop like this, instead of having half of Rajasthan in tow… ha ha. The only respite she provided was when she had to answer this urgent phone call on her cell phone and once again when she visited the washroom.

On those two occasions, the chatty woman's younger brother asked Sneha what she studied, whether she'd been to the US before and where she'd like to go for their honeymoon. Sneha had barely managed replying to these and was about to ask him why he wanted to marry someone a good nine years younger than him, when the sister invaded the conversation.

"Bhai, is there anything else you want to ask Sneha? I think she is the prettiest girl you have ever met. Look at our Delhi girls, so sober, fresh and young looking. Not like the half dressed women in your country! Isn't she just perfect for you?" After that incessant stream of rhetoric questions, the younger brother could offer little more than a benign smile.

Had Sneha not known how serious her parents were about this marital alliance and how her life was to change for good, she would have actually enjoyed this meeting. She would have viewed the encounter with this buxom woman as a source of raw material for the famous mimicry sessions she and Viv indulged in. If she did not have to convey the news of her engagement that evening, she and Viv would have had yet another enjoyable evening, imitating and laughing at the mannerisms of people each of them encountered. But her gregarious prospective sister-in-law was the last person on Sneha's mind when she met Viv that evening. She told him she was getting engaged and he said that's good and wished her all the best… just like that. The two of them had never argued, primarily because they had never expected anything from each other and were not about to start now.

Though she and Viv chatted about everything under the sun, Viv never discussed Sneha with Maya. Sneha was too caught up in "head to toe" preparations for the mega event and Maya barely met her during that three-month whirlwind period. The primary sources of this information were of course, Mitali and Siya. In a rare moment when she dropped her guard and allowed herself to be judgmental and more because she thought she saw pain in Viv's eyes when he kissed Sneha by the pool side that "wedding shower" afternoon, Maya blurted out, "But if Sneha loves Viv so much that she cannot let go of him even on the day of her wedding shower, why didn't she at least try telling her parents about him?"

"Not everyone is lucky enough to be able to marry the person they love, Maya," Siya snapped back icily, the coldness betraying the tinge of sadness that crept in.

"Not a flower beneath the class of carnations Maya, and that was just the wedding. There is a lifetime ahead. Imagine giving up every such thing one has always taken for granted. Imagine giving up a way of life itself," reasoned Mitali.

"And what could Sneha have told her parents? That she will not accept this proposal because she wants to marry this singer cum mimic who works as a disc jockey in a five star pub? That they should entrust her to a man whose annual salary could barely equal the price of a diamond set or two in her Dad's showroom?" continued Siya, upset that Maya had raised the query at all.

"Is that what celebrity break-ups were about?" Maya wondered, realizing that she still had a lot more to learn about what people wanted from life.

7

SUPERWOMAN

As a teenager, Maya knew what she wanted from her own life. Maya was fascinated by class alright, but she was far more taken in by the value of a great marriage. Maya was determined to have a wonderful married life, one that worked and withstood the ravages of children, drudgery, boredom and changing circumstances. And more than anything else, Maya did not want to be the kind of wife her mother had been. She hated her mother because she had seen her squeeze Dad of his self-confidence and pride and she hated him because he let her do it. She observed, absorbed and despised them- day in and day out, while they thought Maya did not know, and did not notice.

It began innocuously enough. Sunayana was home on Saturdays while her husband had alternate Saturdays off. On one such Saturday afternoon, seven-year-old Maya was engrossed in her water colors at the dining table. A client and his wife had dropped in at home to thank Sunayana for her services and congratulate her on the way she had handled the rather tricky case for them.

Sunayana did not encourage clients to visit her at home and Maya knew she was not entirely pleased to see the couple in her drawing room on a Saturday. Anyway, the couple was brimming with gratitude and decency demanded that they be served tea and snacks. Sunayana did the needful and had all the intentions of wrapping up the meeting in 15 minutes, when the telephone rang. Maya jumped up to answer it,

"Hello Dad, I'm painting. I've painted a sunset with black birds flying out near the sun. Dad, if the birds fly out really high, do you think they can go and touch the sun?" Maya knew she could ask Dad the stupidest of questions and he would not laugh. He calmly answered that if they tried hard enough, the birds would reach the sun, but the sun was so hot, may be they didn't really want to go near it and then asked for Sunayana.

The couple, who had come to meet Sunayana really had overstayed and Sunayana was wondering how she could get rid of them. She could have easily used the phone call as an excuse and bid them good bye, but she didn't. She purposely strode up to the telephone and said in an irate "I'm busy" kind of tone, "Haanji? Haan, I have some clients over. Is there anything specific? Nothing na? Don't you have any work at the bank? I'll hang up then," she put the phone down with a flourish, audibly murmuring how her husband called from office for no rhyme or reason and didn't nationalized banks in the country have any clients to service.

"As against that, look at the pressure on the legal profession in this country!" she said, as if she was talking to herself as she came back and settled herself in the sofa before her guests. "Yes Mr Mehra, won't you have some more namkeen…" The Mehras had got the point. Sunayana wore the trousers in this house and liked to show it too. Her husband plodded along in life while she was the success story. Maya was too young to catch on to the nuances of what transpired that afternoon, but the seeds had been sown. Over time, Maya too began to believe in the superior nature of her mother's capabilities as a professional as well as a homemaker.

8
POOR RELATIONS

Bua always wore "wash and wear" nylon saris at home and artificial silk ones for special occasions. Unlike the elegant crisp cottons in pastel shades or black that Sunayana sported in court and the floral prints (again in sober colors) she wore at home, Bua always wore outrageously bright saris. A shocking pink and brown combination or more often, a white or cream sari with a loud print teamed with a white blouse. As a result of this "blatantly lower middle-class dress sense", according to Maya, when Bua came to stay with them in Delhi, Maya was embarrassed to go out with her.

When Bua came visiting, Sunayana had a set routine. Every morning, with her characteristic efficiency, Sunayana would roll out chapatis for Bua's lunch, leave the salad in the refrigerator and the dal and vegetable on the small fold-up breakfast table in the kitchen. She'd pack her own lunch and speed off to work announcing that the work pressure was far too much and that she'd be home late. More often than not, Dad would call in sick or utilize yet another 'casual leave' when they had his sister or any other house guests. Dad would have truly preferred to have Sunayana making time for his only sister especially given that her visits were so rare. But Sunayana and Bua had so little in common that Maya could not imagine what they would say to each other if left alone for too long.

Once Sunayana had left home, Dad would stretch himself over the diwan in the living room. During Delhi's hot summer, Dad would prefer to hang his kurta on the hook in their bedroom and walk about the house wearing his cotton vest and pajamas. This attire was certainly looked down upon by Maya and to a degree of lesser severity by her mother. But Bua naturally had no such notions. She would pick some tasks to be done from Sunayana's immaculately organized kitchen and settle her ample frame on the living room floor. As she squatted on the floor, a plate full of garlic petals to be peeled or rice grains to be cleared before her, the siblings would chat the whole day long.

From the travails of their relations in the small town back home that Bua narrated with aplomb to what the winds of change were doing to today's youth, the two would revel in animated conversation. At periodic intervals, Bua would get up and bring back hot cups of tea for both of them – another habit that Sunayana did not like to encourage in her husband.

When Maya came home from school, she had the dual treat of Dad and Bua's presence instead of letting herself in with her own set of keys. Maya didn't really mind walking into an empty house every evening. Sunayana being so particular, Maya's after-school snack was always placed at the corner of the breakfast table in the kitchen neatly covered with a white napkin. A mug of cold chocolate milk was in the refrigerator, always on the top right corner of the first level after the deep freeze compartment, so that Maya could locate it instantly. The part-time maid's unplanned absence, a client calling up in the midst of her rolling rotis or the morning alarm not ringing in time … Irrespective of domestic calamities like these every morning, Sunayana always managed to accomplish it all.

Not a day had passed when Maya's after-school snack was not in place or her milk had not been poured out. Not a day without all three of their lunch boxes packed with fresh, soft rotis and vegetables (no short-cut with sandwiches or snacks from the market) laid out and ready before 9 a.m. Whatever time

Maya

Sunayana returned from work, she'd toss up a delicious meal within half an hour, the maid having kneaded the dough and chopped the vegetables in the morning. Whatever had transpired at court during the day never seemed to sap Sunayana's energy. As soon as she walked in, the sequence of events would be this- her sandals would quickly settle themselves on the designated slot on the shoe-rack, her empty tiffin box opened and into the sink, promptly aired and watered so as to avoid foul smells. Her handbag would go in the steel cupboard and the files she brought home to read, on the wooden shelf. She'd quickly wash her face and hands and step into the kitchen.

The pressure cooker with rice and dal would go up on one stove first. The chopped vegetables would be tossed in a pan on the other stove. As she'd wait for the pressure built up in the cooker to simmer down, she'd quickly grind fresh green chutney in the electronic mixer or toss up a boondi raita. The vegetable done by now, would be transferred to a serving bowl, the tadka for the dal in the same *dekchi*. (not just saving up on soap to wash extra utensils but also gaining negotiating power with the part-time maid on the approximate number of utensils to be washed every morning). As the dal simmered on one side, Sunayana would deftly roll out seven rotis for the three of them- the entire exercise complete in 35 minutes flat.

Not surprisingly, Sunayana had little patience with people who worked hard instead of smart and no respect for the typical Indian housewife claim that food cooked on "a slow fire with all the love, care and patience of a mother," resulted in superior taste. This was one of the several reasons Sunayana resented the presence of her sister-in-law in her home. Bua would spend hours in her kitchen, labouring on her brother's favorite dishes and mess up Sunayan's kitchen in the process. Kitchen titles sputtered with turmeric and oil used for deep frying paneer and cauliflower pakoras, Sunayana's otherwise gleaming gas stove with tell-tale signs of chickpea flour batter and the kitchen platform sticky with sugar-syrup from the sweets she made.

This afternoon, when Maya returned from school, Bua welcomed her with a plate of kachoris and steaming hot *besan ka halwa*, as Dad looked on indulgently. It gave Dad great pride to see Maya enjoying the efforts of his own kin.

When Maya was younger, a few days at Bua's house had been fun during the Diwali holidays. Sunayana never accompanied them citing the work that had piled up. Still, Bua's letter arrived dutifully, every *bhaidooj* and *rakhee* (both festivals celebrating the affectionate bond between a brother and a sister), inviting all three of them to spend a few days with her family.

Bua's Diwali preparations would begin days in advance, rolling out *mathris* by the kilo, stirring large tins full of halwa and laying out rows of bright yellow *boondi laddoos* on sparkling stainless steel plates. Dad, who was reticent and rather unsure of himself in Delhi, would blossom into a jovial, magnanimous "favorite uncle" in Bua's house.

Despite the inevitable tongue clicking and head shaking by Sunayana, Dad would pack his suitcase with trinkets for the multitude of relatives back home. As he showed off pretty little Maya to them, the multitude of aunts, uncles, and cousins would shower her with gifts too. A bright purple and green artificial silk dress with flounces, red plastic sandals with shiny bows and a charming toy kitchen set -- Maya would bring back her treasures to Delhi with delight... until class consciousness set in.

As childhood slipped into adolescence, Maya refused to accompany Dad on these hometown sojourns. Some of her extremely well-to-do friends at school went off on holidays abroad, flaunting fancy electronic gadgets and branded apparel on their return. With growing frustration at her parent's limited means and outlook, Maya preferred to say she went nowhere during her holidays rather than a decidedly lower middle class small town.

9

A CHANGE OF FORTUNE

In this shunning of Dad's relatives, Maya had Sunayana's whole-hearted support; for Sunayana would rather hob-nob with her own relatives on 'foreign shores'.

Once, Sunayana's brother had suggested to her that Maya's Dad could find opportunities in the accounts section of the company he worked in Bahrain. The money would no doubt be much better and Dad would finally grow out of his stagnating job. Bua's husband (Maya's Phuphaji) and son Suketu were in Delhi then, having dropped in for a day to enquire about computer courses for Suketu after his Standard 10 board examinations.

Like most sensitive and sensible women would, Sunayana could have chosen to broach the subject of this "proposed job change" in the privacy of their bedroom. But Sunayana, with her characteristic tactlessness, coupled may be with insensitivity mixed with malice, chose the very public setting for this discussion- the foldable dining table in their small but neat kitchen. Suketu, his father and Dad were having dinner. Maya had eaten already and was doing her homework in her bedroom. Sunayana introduced the subject as she began serving the hot rotis she had just rolled.

A Change of Fortune

"Some siblings are so close, they love each other so much that they could do anything for each other," said Sunayana as she dabbed homemade *ghee* on to the *rotis* before serving them. Dad and Phuphaji continued to eat, wondering what this was about.

"It is not that bank employees the world over are badly paid. If you have the opportunity, and more important, the ambition to do something for your family, you can live in the Gulf and change your life!" said Sunayana. Dad continued to eat quietly, but Phuphaji ventured,

" Chhoti bhabhi what are you saying? What is this about?"

"Oh Jijaji everything is so expensive in Delhi, it is not like living in a small town you know. Maya goes to one of the best schools in the city. I had to take on two extra cases so that we could manage the fees in a lump sum. Life here is so difficult, so much money for every little thing. You can see me slaving night and day. How do I say it Jijaji, but sometimes I feel that being a housewife would have been a better option. But as if I have the luxury like Didi! You bring in enough money so that Didi can concentrate on her job of bringing up Suketu and minding your home."

The sob story was attaining a vivid, colourful form and Dad had stopped eating. Sunayana got up to serve warm rice and dal, purposefully adding extra dollops of ghee on the mounds of fluffy white rice on the two plates.

"Lo ji, it is your favorite dal, laced with cream, just the way you like it," she said to Dad, smiling sweetly at Phuphaji, engrossed in her "sweet wife-great home-maker" act. Dad as usual, said nothing. Later, in his sole moment of rebellion and rage, Dad was to liken this particular episode to that of a chicken in a slaughterhouse,

"Stuff the wretched bird with great food, fatten it, wash it with care and carefully prick it."

Maya remembered how she had caught the entire exchange between Mom and Phupaji as she pretended to finish her homework. Completely ignoring Dad except to heap more food on to his plate, Sunayana had vividly described the morbidity of circumstances that had forced her to "slog like a bullock by day and nurture like a cow as evening set in." She then dwelt on how her brother was ready to offer Dad a position in the accounts department of his company in Bahrain, how the money would be excellent and there would be ample saving for Maya's education and wedding as well. The job demanded that Dad stay in Bahrain for eight months at a stretch and he would then be able to visit India for a month. Opportunities for children's education were limited and Sunayana would have no legal practice there, so the two of them would stay back in Delhi.

Dinner done, Dad washed his hands, went into the bedroom and sat down with Maya. Maya, wide-eyed and confused was still trying to pretend that she had heard nothing. The rage that Sunayana's dramatic outburst had built up could well have resulted in a verbal, if not violent duel between any other husband and wife. But Dad never expressed his anger, either to Sunayana, Phuphaji, Maya or anyone else. He sat beside little Maya, stroking her hair gently.

10

DEATH OF A SUPERWOMAN

However intense the provocation, Dad never retaliated, except on that fateful day. And when he finally did, it was all over… just like that. Thirty odd years of chipping away at this ego had sharpened the broken edges to such an extent that the chiseled edge could draw blood. That mean streak in her, the long nights when she tortured him, whetting his desire to frenzy and then depriving him of the sexual pleasure that years of conditioning had told him, was his due; the years of asides and insults she flung at him boiled to the brim during that moment of rage.

Maya and Rahul were in Singapore when it happened. Rahul was on a six-month assignment, "scoping a software project" and simultaneously building contacts for future deals for a small, but sound Chennai - based software company. Much to Maya's relief, the laid-back, fun-loving, almost flighty boy of their college days was transforming into a true professional, driven to outperform and succeed. But the obsession with work that blinded him to all else later in life was still to set in.

For when Suketu's crackling voice on the overseas call pulled him out of a client meeting, the client's reaction occupied no mind space in his stunned

Maya

brain. "But what happened? Mummyji spoke to Maya just a week ago I think. She had no major health problems as far as I know. Has there been a road accident? How has Maya's father taken it..." Rahul sputtered, trying to figure out how we would break the news to Maya.

"No no, it happened at home. Mamaji is, not... not here. It was not a painful death, tell Maya please. When should I come to the airport to pick her up? My mother was saying you have important work and you may not be able to come." Suketu would say no more.

"We'll be on the first flight to Delhi available. And we'll come home on our own, Rahul said, stuffing the notes of his interrupted meeting inside the folder. Back in the conference room, the client delegation stared at him, grim, more than a little annoyed at the interruption in the meeting. Before the head of the delegation could get in a word, Rahul said, his voice sober, "I am extremely sorry for the inconvenience caused to you gentlemen. There has been an untimely death in my family and I need to fly to India at the earliest. My colleague Raman will take this forward. Please be assured that Raman will have access to all our previous communication regarding this project." Rahul stepped out of the cold room; acutely aware of the precarious position he had placed his professional life in.

"In their frenzied efforts to impress, Indian software professionals over the years had projected themselves as workaholics, willing to bend backwards to meet the client's demands and with zilch personal commitment," he thought. If, God forbid, someone from the client delegation had had to leave the meeting due to a personal tragedy, Rahul knew he would have been understanding and would have even offered to take on additional responsibility in order to ease the burden on the affected party. But, his views on the softer issues involving the Indian software services industry could wait. Top priority was a call to his Indian boss in Chennai, a handover meeting with Raman and then home to Maya.

As expected, the boss in Chennai was indifferent to his situation, but keen on knowing what the client had to say. Raman, eager to please, vigorously nodded to all that Rahul had to say. How he would actually handle the project, would be visible in the days to come. Another two calls later, Rahul booked Maya and himself on the next flight to Delhi, 10 hours away.

11

CEO MATERIAL

For someone who would rather have had a child than more money to do his MBA, for someone who chucked the Singapore assignment so that he could be with Maya on the painful flight to her mother's funeral, Rahul had come a long way. There were no small pleasures any more.

Having long abandoned his scruffy jeans and T-shirts with whacky graffiti and long locks emulating his favourite rock star, Rahul was now a mobile advertisement for designer formal wear. Crisp, branded shirts, elegant jackets, ties in striking colours and socks in shades that precisely matched the colour tone and texture of finely cut trousers.

Well turned out, distinguished looking, the corner office, secretary, frequent overseas travel, networking events, appearances on business programmes on television and profiled in business magazines, Rahul was every bit the high flying husband Maya had dreamt he would be.

When Maya first met Rahul, his 'chilled out' self, 'habit of hanging out', 'floater' personality and instability could well have been a subconscious attempt to disguise his loneliness. Rahul never spoke about his family to anyone and given that his origins were equally 'middle-class' and in fact 'small-town middle-class' compared to Maya's Delhi upbringing, Maya did not want to raise them either.

Maya and Rahul first met a few years after the death of his parents and younger sister Ritu in a bus accident. Rahul's father had been a schoolteacher and his mother had taken up embroidery to supplement the family's humble income. Rahul would have grown up in small town Ambala and attended the Hindi medium school his father taught in, had it not been for his father's fierce ambition to give his children a better education compared to what he had access to. Supported by his uneducated but extremely hardworking wife, Ramprasad Sikand enrolled his son in the only English medium school that existed in Ambala. Bright, with a natural affinity for science and maths, Rahul passed his board exams with flying colours and won a community scholarship to study engineering at a college in Delhi. The family was overjoyed.

Much to Rahul's disappointment, the bright Ambala topper was now just a nonentity. The hostile urbanized Delhi college crowd looked down upon him as a 'small-town nerd' and the hostel food was tasteless… there was nothing he liked about his new life. After weeks of moping about, solace came in the form of a new room-mate Shanky. Footloose and fancy free and brimming over with self-confidence, Shanky pulled the reticent Rahul out of his shell and into his bunch of friends living on the edge.

Rahul's scholarship had covered tuition fees, the cost of books and study equipment. His hostel fees and living expenses still needed to be taken care of. But Ramprasad would never accept defeat. He decided to sell off the asset hoarded for his daughter Ritu's education and wedding expenses – a patch of ancestral agricultural land. Before Ramprasad set off with his wife and daughter for the village, he called Rahul,

"Beta, I thought it would be nice for all of us to visit the family deity after the land deal is signed. The patch of land was our last connection with my ancestors. But don't worry about not being able to come along with us. Ritu's just finished her exams and it will be a good trip for her. God willing, she too will join you in Delhi some day. You just study hard and don't worry about anything else," Ramprasad finished his last conversation with Rahul.

The next Rahul heard of his family was 12 hours later when their neighbour in Ambala called his hostel room at midnight. The bus carrying the Sikands and 27 other passengers had skid off the mountain track plunging into the valley. There were just six survivors fighting for their lives in a government hospital. Sadly, nobody from his family had made it. With no mobile phones, little identification on the mangled bodies and the chaos at the hospital, it had been hours before families could be contacted and bodies claimed. Shell-shocked, Rahul made the arduous bus journey home alone.

The well-meaning neighbours had contacted his relatives from nearby villages and when Rahul got home, he had to mechanically follow the instructions of a retired Uncle who had assumed charge of the arrangements. Too much of a macho man already to shed a tear, Rahul lit the funeral pyres of his father, mother and sister in silence, the Sanskrit chants of the priest drumming in his ears. As per his Uncle's instructions, Rahul stayed in the house for the next fortnight. Neighbours brought in food at mealtimes and Uncle kept vigil to keep the oil lamps lit in memory of his family aglow. On the day of the prayer ceremony, Rahul, dressed in white, his arms folded in a Namaste mutely nodded to the visitors as they came in to pay their respects. The next morning, his Uncle went back to his village.

And then there was silence. Rahul returned to his hostel room in Delhi having shut off the home that reminded him of the only people he had known closely and loved. Rahul never returned to Ambala again.

Shanky had no interest whatsoever in engineering or grades and had landed in the engineering college via the management quota. Rahul's grades too began to suffer. And the topper from Ambala barely scraped through the engineering college exams at first attempt. Campus placement passed him by and Rahul drifted along in the Shanky league, this time trying out a multitude of business ideas none of which ever took off. From cyber cafes and pool tables to bottled exotic vegetables and managing music events, Shanky and Rahul tried everything and failed. Eventually, Shanky was packed off to Australia by his parents.

With the venture capital dried up, Rahul had no choice but to set his entrepreneurial ego aside and take up a job as a junior programmer in a small but stable software services company. As soon as the six-month probation period was over and Rahul got his confirmation letter along with a marginal salary raise, Maya and Rahul were at her parents' doorstep, seeking their blessings. Maya's mother was sorely disappointed, still appalled by Maya's decision to chuck her architecture career and her choice of husband.

"With Maya's good looks and consistent academic performance, she could have done so much better on all counts," she rued.

Maya ignored the insinuation and simply announced that she and Rahul would be at the court the next morning.

"Rahul made an application with the marriage registrar four weeks ago as per law. I am above 18 and the law gives me the right to get married," she declared without raising her voice.

Nobody knew Indian law better than Sunayana and she knew there was nothing she could do to stop Maya. But there was no law against fretting and fuming! And she did. Her spiteful monologue encompassed the historical lethargy in her husband's ancestral make-up, the social circumstances two decades ago that gave even highly educated women like her no choice but to accept the marital alliance their parents chose for them and the resultant life of drudgery, intense hard work that she had suffered all her life.

"But you had a choice Maya and this is what you chose. Do you not have any aspirations beyond the sad peeling paint of the ancient block of flats we've lived in!" Sunayana concluded her outburst with a dramatic sigh and a flow of tears. Maya did not bother explaining her aspirations to her mother and walked out of the room rolling her eyes at Rahul. Rahul followed.

Newly married, Rahul struggled with his job as Maya struggled with hers at the lawyer's office. Finally, it was the Executive MBA in Singapore and the campus placement it offered that kick-started Rahul's career.

Over the years, Rahul had transformed into a 24X7 professional, fiercely competitive, a go-getter, who would do anything to achieve what he believed should be his. He seemed to thrive on stress and the adrenaline rush of photo finish wins. Anointed Chief Executive of an IT company floated by one of India's oldest and largest business groups, Rahul was the blue-eyed boy of the company's Board of Directors. The Board's chairman septuagenarian Lala Manmalchand described Rahul as *'honhaar bachha'* (able kid). He happily left the company's strategy, sales, marketing, operations and the award-receiving to Rahul and was content to sit back and enjoy the fruits of his investment. Rahul thrived on the freedom. After years of breaking his back in towing a line he didn't completely believe in, finally, this was an opportunity to implement all that his expensive executive MBA programme and the years on the field had taught him.

There was no day, no night anymore. "Operational excellence, strategic initiative, innovation, people engagement, customer delight..." the corporate terminology ran thick and fast in every 'high-level' meeting, every conference discussion. In the virtual war-rooms he had created, the troops were raring to go, and Rahul would spare no effort to meet the ambitious goals he had set. In fact, riding on the wave of success, he wanted himself and his team to over-achieve the stretch targets.

On the home front of course, everything that needed to be done in order to keep the wheels of their life turning smoothly was done by Maya and with great aplomb. Rahul had not stepped into Maya's immaculate super-equipped kitchen for years. Maya's well turned out and loyal 'staff' would have fainted at the very idea of Sahib having to lift a finger! During Rahul and Maya's newly married years Maya would encourage Rahul to help out around the house and he would. Those were the days of Maya's stressful law firm job and part-time help eating into limited finances. But as Rahul grew in professional stature and Maya became a chauffeur driven kitty party hopping Madamji, instances of Rahul's entry into the kitchen diminished and eventually stopped completely. Even when the 'staff' had their time off or Rahul was working late, Maya would have an appetizing meal on the table, carefully laid out.

CEO Material

Whatever the time when Rahul would turn the key into the lock and try to sneak in so as to not wake up Maya, she would be waiting up in bed in her soft pastel nightgown. Of late he would walk in with the Bluetooth device tucked behind his ear still battling the vagaries of his teams across continents. He would mumble he'd eaten and that she should go to sleep. She'd quietly put the dinner away and have his nightcap at the bedside and try to catch some sleep.

During the initial days of his travel, Maya would diligently be at the airport to receive him especially after he was returning from an overseas trip. When he had to travel at short notice, she'd have all that he needed laid out on the bed for him. Rahul always preferred to pack himself. "So that I know exactly where things are and don't have to rummage through stuff before rushing for a meeting," he would say.

But there it all was, piles of shirts, trousers, ties, neatly ironed, pairs of socks perfectly matching with each set of trousers, cologne, aftershave, small pouches of dry fruits if he ever needed a power-snack, even a light book in case he felt like he needed a to relax. But Rahul did not read fiction any more. He preferred business magazines.

In the initial days when Rahul first started making business trips abroad, Maya and Rahul would excitedly plan to travel together. "My company's paying for my ticket any way Maya. If you come along and we pay for yours, we can effectively have an overseas holiday at half the cost," Rahul would say, taking a few days off after the business meetings were over. Delighted, Maya would have the itinerary worked out; looking up cosy, budget hotels to move to once Rahul's official business days were over and the real holiday began. They had explored Paris together this way, losing their way, taking the wrong bus, sampling strange sounding exotic dishes off the menu… Tourists they befriended on these trips would sometimes mistake them for honeymooners or the rare Indian couple taking a holiday without the kids to celebrate a milestone anniversary.

Maya

But Maya did not even realize when these trips stopped. She need not even have looked up budget hotels and cheap air tickets any more; the perquisites of Rahul's position would have covered it all. But at some point, Rahul started brushing away suggestions of Maya travelling saying he had to rush back to Delhi for an important presentation with Lala Manmalchand, a board meeting or a media interaction planned months in advance.

This was actually true. For the freedom to run the company as he pleased came with the rider that if Lalaji wished to see him and wanted the company's financial displayed, there was no option but for Rahul to present himself in the red and gold adorned room. Trying to have anyone else from his team for such crucial appearances could prove disastrous. For the breath of hesitance in quoting revenue and profit numbers would see Lalaji's gnarled fingers tighten around the carved lion's mane on his royal wooden chair.

"You are learned people with foreign management degrees. All this PR, strategy, advertising I do not want to know. But the munafa (profit) should be in your head, not hidden inside this electronic *chopdi* (notebook traditionally used to keep accounts)," he would say softly, the fingers of his right palm brushing away non-existent dust from his creamy white dhoti. Rahul knew that very few, in fact, no-one in his team, had the sensitivity to grasp the chilling warning hidden in Lalaji's benign smile.

But then, such a pressing engagement back in Delhi was not the only reason for Rahul to brush away Maya's suggestion of travelling with him. For now, Malathy was on the radar.

12

GREEN – THE COLOR OF PAIN

She knew he loved someone else… loved her from the bottom of his heart, with his entire being, in an intense, all consuming way. She thought sex had little to do with it, or may be it did. She knew he loved the other woman because he had once loved her the very same way. Not so very long ago or so she thought. The fact that she was a nubile teenager when she met him years ago seemed to evade her consciousness. To her, it still seemed like yesterday.

"Do I need a husband? Do I need a man in my life? I never thought of it like that and maybe it is not 'cool' to think like that but I think I do need Rahul in my life."

It had been a few years since Maya repeatedly had this conversation with herself. The frequency of these thoughts had increased lately, especially since Malathy came into the picture or rather, in Maya's line of vision.

Maya had denied it to herself for months, even after that gross lipstick mark on Rahul's tie after he came back from his Bangalore trip. But the instant Maya saw Malathy for the first time and the way Rahul looked at her; she knew they were in love. Maya felt this deep, throbbing pain, almost like someone had physically whacked her on the chest. It dulled her senses and moistened the corners of her carefully done up eyes.

Malathy was a classic Indian 'working mother'. In fact, in a lot of ways, Maya was reminded of her own mother when she saw Malathy. Malathy was Sunayana's efficiency, her zest for life, sans her maliciousness. When Rahul met Malathy, or rather, when she joined the company he headed, she was already a mother of two boys- four and seven years old. What attracted Rahul to her initially was her air of quiet confidence, the ease with which she carried herself in simple, bright coloured saris and a face that masked a stressful work life and Rahul was to know later, a lonely personal one.

Malathy usually wore almost no make-up— just a touch of kohl, which she often did not bother to touch up during the day, and a bare hint of lipstick. With her husband on the ship nearly nine months a year, Malathy had opted to live in a house next to her parents.

"Greatly convenient" she said, for the kids could run back and forth between the two houses whenever she worked late and the four of them could still be on their own whenever her husband Pradeep was in town.

It all started with the discovery that both Malathy and Rahul preferred to work late instead of getting in early, and that both of them loved masala tea. If it had not been for Rahul's perseverance and the overwhelming possessiveness he felt about Malathy, things would have stopped right there. If someone would have told Malathy that she would end up living in with her boss, she would have laughed her head off.

"I am a happily married mother of two, thank you. And that big shot Rahul Sikand! He may be a big boss around here and is quite pleasant to chat with. But he's not my type- too shy, she would have dismissed the suggestion with her characteristic tinkling laughter. She would have been right, but for text messaging. The mobile phone had virtually become an extension of Rahul's arm and the text message, the perfect mode of communication for the man of few words. The otherwise reticent Rahul's ardour flourished as he typed out all that he wanted to convey to Malathy. Charmed by his wit and passionate play of words that slipped so easily into the void in her life, Malathy did not resist.

ENCOUNTER

13

ENCOUNTER

There was an aspect of Sunayana's persona that Maya did not mind inheriting – playing the part of a perfect hostess. But unlike Sunayana's occasional dinners hosted in the confines of her modest drawing room, Maya's 'do's' were lavish, unforgettable events for her guests and a source of envy for those who were not invited. With her trained staff of six and additional well-turned out backup of another 10, Maya's dinner parties, musical evenings and traditional *pooja* lunches easily saw a guest list of 100 or more. Being meticulous and class conscious, Maya displayed disdain for anyone who tried to pass off biryani in aluminium foil or fiery hot 'Indian' noodles in polythene containers as dinner for guests.

In Maya's home, every occasion for entertaining guests was viewed as a potential networking opportunity for Rahul and herself and the efforts that went into organizing each of these do's can only be described as perfection personified. A pooja meant that Maya's exquisite traditional saris, collection of ornate jewellery and handpicked set of silver prayer ritual paraphernalia got a public viewing. In keeping with the colour scheme of Maya's sari, a finely embroidered kurta and a shawl or jacket would be laid out for Rahul. Almost mechanically and despite back-to-back meetings, Rahul would appear at the pooja dressed in the outfit Maya had had dutifully laid out for him.

Apart from the regularly updated guest list on Maya's computer, there was another list that no-one knew existed – a meticulously maintained chronicle of the menu at each of these do's along with a note on what she and Rahul were wearing on the occasion! Maya would wince when she encountered the same old appetizers at the nth party hosted by one of Rahul's associates and shake her head in disbelief when she saw another re-cycling a gold and blue scarf on a third outfit. Maya wanted no such goof-ups for Rahul and herself. It was a matter of class after all.

It was at one such mega-bash that Maya first set her eyes on Malathy. Though she had been working with Rahul's company for fairly long, she was not really part of the 'inner circle' or the 'must invite' list Maya procured from Rahul's personal assistant. This time, Malathy's name had slipped in. One, she had been promoted recently and two, she seemed to be part of the cc list for important official events within the company (those that did not include spouses).

The occasion for Maya's bash this time, was that Maya wanted to give a break to a contemporary fusion music band from Mumbai. The guitarist and pop singer had cut a melodious but not so popular music album. They had now teamed up with a lavani folk singer from Maharashtra to create contemporary 'Mystic magic' with a fusion album. The guitarist's brother had been an ally during Maya's frenetic social climbing days and she was returning a favour by agreeing to host the trio at a performance for select but influential guests at her sprawling home.

In keeping with the 'remix' theme for the evening, Maya's able team had transformed their expansive living room into a nightclub. The bar in the corner served cocktails with names borrowed from the latest remix numbers, the walls were lined with screens displaying a blend of old world cinema and the fiery, albeit raunchy pace of the new.

The tastefully laid out menu too saw the creative blend of two eras – fluffy idlis with a crunchy lamb mince mix tucked into a triangle carved into the round rice dumpling, a wild remix salad comprising roasted nuts, boiled shell macaroni, burnished cottage cheese cubes straight out of the tandoor oven and fried strips of marinated chicken. Maya usually looked down upon the generous but unimaginative hostesses like Charu Batra who served the standard North Indian Mutter Paneer, Rajma and Palak Paneer at every meal and also punctuated the spread with an irrelevant and un-co-ordinated non-starter like Gobi Manchurian or Paneer *Au gratin*! But today, the remix theme had given Maya the license to break her own rules on suitability of mixing cuisines while planning menus. So just like it was with everything that Maya did, it was a perfectly planned evening.

And exactly as per her usual plan, Maya's trained team apprised her on the completion of their assignments as per schedule – food, drinks, décor, acoustics and so on. Suitably satisfied that everything was just the way it should be, at 6 pm, Maya slipped into her bubble bath to ready herself for the eventful evening.

At 8 pm, when she emerged on the lawns, nobody could have believed that she had spent the day on her toes supervising every detail to ensure that the scene was perfect. She was dressed in navy blue silk flared trousers and a slinky sleeveless top with a gold streak across the back. A shimmering gold and blue silk and chiffon dupatta slung across her left shoulder gave a stunning ethnic effect to the otherwise Westernized outfit. Classy but simple, she wore a thin platinum chain around her neck with a sapphire and diamond encrusted pendant. Her earlobes twinkled with tiny sapphires set in platinum. As always, before she left the bedroom, she had laid out an elegant kurta in the same colour scheme for Rahul.

But Rahul was not home yet and the guests would soon begin to trickle in. Rahul's long work hours, his cellphone going on voice mail and barely making it in time for social events was not new to Maya. She had developed the poise to never admonish him in public or even when they were alone with each other. In fact, she went great lengths to defend his absence citing

Encounter

the critical professional responsibilities he shouldered. Given Maya's charm and natural grace in the public interaction arena, she was tackling his absence well yet another time. But when Rahul happened to be the host and 15 of the early birds had already taken their seats on the lawns, it hurt that Rahul had not bothered making it in time. Then, one of his colleagues tactlessly remarked that Rahul's cabin had been locked all evening when he rushed home from work to get dressed and make it in time. It was a morbid moment! Maya was seething, but she smiled, ready to hold her own with, "Oh Rahul had a client meeting at the Taj and was to come straight home thereafter. Delhi traffic I tell you!"

This, after Maya had got the PA to block Rahul's calendar for the event weeks in advance and had reminded him about it the same morning, it was so demeaning, she felt so small.

The 'networking hour' over the snazzy cocktails and delicious appetizers was drawing to a close. Running out of excuses to delay the performance, Maya was about to step on to the dais when Rahul walked in, along with a lady Maya did not recognize.

"Sorry people, Malathy and I were on a T-con and the Japs just wouldn't let go. After 90 challenging minutes, one is still left wondering whether the interpreter really conveyed what we were trying to get across," grinned Rahul, slipping into a chair, loosening his tie over a crumpled shirt. He shot Maya an apologetic look with the full confidence that she would understand... work occupied the top slot in his life, yet another time.

Too upset and too dignified to indulge in a slanging match in public, Maya blinked back the tears that threatened to emerge, took a deep breath and stepped on to the dais to introduce the artists for the evening.

14

LETTING GO

As a child Maya had never displayed much of an attachment to any of the series of modest flats that she and her parents had lived in. They just never seemed hers. Today, as her personal belongings (things that Maya valued but Rahul didn't really care for) were packed in a row of smart cases, Maya felt deep pain at being wrenched away from the home she and Rahul had built bit by bit. The bit by bit was certainly not due to financial constraints as Rahul and Maya were at the peak of their financial success when they bought this sprawling six-bedroom mansion.

With a sense of regret that transcended the significant material value of each aesthetic possession, Maya stared bleary eyed at all that she had lost – Suddenly, the beautiful home, its possessions and her status as Mrs. Sikand seemed insignificant before the big loss – of the love, companionship, friendship, care and the focus of her existence for all her adult life – Rahul.

Her gaze wandered around the bookcases, Rahul's industry awards, the various artefacts they had picked up during trips abroad and Maya's own paintings. There was a small water colour of a beautiful white bird poised to take flight. Maya had painted it for Rahul when he went off to Singapore to pursue his

Letting Go

MBA ... of course the bird signified Rahul. Another series of three small pencil sketches had just two hands on each sheet of paper— the first had a child's plump fingers entwined with sinuous masculine ones, the second had the two hands together in a joyous high-five and the third had the two hands that seemed to inch close to each other but still too far apart to touch.

As a child, Maya used to be a prolific artiste, her pencil sketches, colourful crayon strokes and water colour creations had adorned every wall of her room, stuck to the refrigerator with a magnet and some even found their way to the cosy space under the glass slab across her Dad's work table at office. Even as he diligently poured over numbers, cleared his 'in tray' and piled up his 'out tray', a glimpse of the plump yellow ducklings wearing baby pink bow ties and Maya's childish scroll "Ducky's day out" would lighten up doting Dad's eyes under his thick spectacles.

"Architecture is a natural choice. At least it gets you a job and pays bills," Sunayana had pronounced when the time came for Maya to choose a career. "Painting and all that is fine for a rich man's wife. You've got to be able to stand on your own two feet. You never know what life has in store for you. Look at me, where would we be if I didn't have my law degree!" she declared as she swiftly dismissed Maya's ideas of going to a fine arts school to pursue a course in 'World painting styles and sculpture'.

Dad could say nothing. He always wanted Maya to have the best but Sunayana was right. Despite the struggle of the last two decades, they were still adding up numbers to be able to give Maya a decent wedding. It was time for Maya to work towards being independent. Hobbies and passion for art would have to wait.

The easels and paintbrushes were stowed away. Even after she and Rahul were married, she barely had time to balance her lawyer assistant job, housework and the drudgery of the commute, to pick up a paint brush. Later, when Rahul's career flourished and Maya finally became the socialite Mrs. Sikand she'd yearned for all her life, she'd been sucked into the social circuit such that art seemed to have lost its charm except to "collect famous painters as good investment."

Back to the present, Maya gathered the set of old paintings to pack. She had this inexplicable desire to pull down her favourite chandelier from the lobby. The piece was far too gaudy to adorn any other home Maya would ever own or live in. But she wanted it down, for she was convinced that Rahul was far too deep in the stupor of Malathy's relationship to ever notice or value the absence of the exquisite artefact that Maya had custom-made so lovingly for their dream home.

Not just the grand chandelier but even the little things Maya had collected did not deserve Rahul's apathy," thought Maya. Maya had been trying to deny Malathy's presence in Rahul's life. By not thinking about it, by not acknowledging the change in Rahul's behaviour, she had thought she could wish it away. Over the past months Rahul had of course vehemently denied that there was anyone else in his life besides Maya and had emphasized that every absence of his must be attributed to the pressing demands of his sky-rocketing career. But Malathy and Rahul's joint appearance at the music event, the lame excuses and the subtle but knowing expressions of his colleagues had shown that people in the room knew what Maya had suspected. And worse, Rahul too seemed to know they knew and did not care!

Even as Maya played the perfect hostess at her otherwise perfect musical evening, she noticed Rahul's frequent lingering glances at Malathy and Malathy's furtive and coy ones. At the end of the performance, Maya proposed the vote of thanks. As the applause died down and people veered towards the food and drinks counters, Maya made her way across the lawns, pausing at every huddled group, politely enquiring whether each one had enjoyed the performance, urging them to help themselves to the appetizers and how thankful she was to have their support for upcoming musicians. Rahul did not join her having stepped into the house to attend yet another phone call from work.

A congregation of suited men was clinking glasses over an animated discussion about the dance of the dollar-rupee exchange rate and its impact on software export companies. A gathering of women was drooling over someone's new diamond set. Some of the couples were exchanging notes with other couples about holidays taken, holidays planned and how they must have the other couple over soon, it really had been so long, they only seemed to be meeting at Maya's dos. In the almost entirely 'heterosexual couples' guest list, Malathy seemed to be the only single person around. At the edge of the garden, Malathy stood alone with her back to the gathering, her laptop bag slung across her shoulder appearing to be engrossed in admiring the arrangement of fairy lights, scented candles and intricately carved terra cotta lamps Maya had placed among the rose bushes. In her simple cotton 'office wear' full sleeved salwar kameez, she looked out of place among the snazzy chiffon sarees and designer outfits of the other women at the party. She seemed to know no-one, except some of her male colleagues who seemed to have veered away from her for some reason. Malathy's proximity to Rahul and the preferential treatment she received from him had caused adequate tongue wagging and resentment and there was nothing like a stray comment made at a social occasion like this to fuel further gossip! Maybe they found it safer to be seen standing closer to their wives or with their own homogenous all-male groups?

Maya walked towards Malathy's lone figure with the intention of introducing her to some of the other guests and asking her to help herself at the food counters. Maya was just a few steps behind Malathy when she realized that Malathy was actually speaking on the phone. She was about to turn away when she heard Rahul's unmistakable voice shouting through the phone line.

"Maly, with you in charge of delivery I shouldn't have to deal with such emergency customer calls! You should have at least warned me that the Singapore interim delivery is delayed. I had to pretend I was aware of the situation. This is so embarrassing!" The otherwise mild-mannered Rahul was fuming, giving Malathy no opportunity to explain her side of the story, whatever it was. There really was nothing inappropriate about the content of the conversation so far, but the tone he used and the underlying sense of familiarity ran a shiver down Maya's spine. It was a tone he had used with no-one else so far except with his own wife. Or so she had thought.

"We have it under control. Everything is ready for delivery but Subu had sent them some queries about the packaging and hosting. He's got a call with their tech lead tomorrow. Once we have clarity on exactly how they want the packaging done, we can deliver within 2 business days. I'm sorry Rahul. I had thought I'd update you on Singapore first thing tomorrow morning. Honestly didn't think he'd break protocol and ring you so late in the evening!" Malathy explained in a soft, even tone.

Rahul's voice softened, "Well, this is what being accessible and customer centric means! Anyway, I have promised him you'd have a detailed update for him first thing tomorrow morning. I've also told him you'll personally accompany the project manager to Singapore for the hand over next month. And I'll bring forward my sales calls to be in Singapore at the same time. Let's do a dinner meeting with him. He'll be pacified at least for the time being! And Maly, love you!"

"Love you Rahul…" Malathy turned around, her bashful smile turning to horror as she saw Maya standing right behind her. Maya had been rooted to the ground unable to control the flow of tears that rolled down silently. Regaining her composure, Maya walked away without a second glance at Malathy. She strode past the cackling kitty party women who had gone silent having witnessed the encounter and were now pretending they had heard nothing. Maya disappeared into the house to freshen up. There were over a 100 guests to be seen off before she would finally see Rahul alone for a watershed conversation that would change their lives forever.

During that largely one-sided conversation, Maya had wept uncontrollably all night asking Rahul what more she could have done to keep their marriage together. Rahul sat silent on the other side of the bed, his face impassive. The tears gave way to a plea; a glimpse of Maya's diminishing self-confidence, "We can still make it Rahul. I don't know when and where we moved apart but we can still make our marriage work. I don't even remember when we last had an argument. If this is not compatibility, what is? Take some time off, let's go away somewhere and not club that with work. Let's see a counsellor. I'm willing to do whatever it takes, just one thing, you need to promise me you'll never see Malathy again."

Letting Go

Rahul finally broke his silence, "Malathy cannot go away from my life and I'd suggest you don't either. You have everything you need and more. Besides, as you said, we too have a good relationship, there is nothing to argue about. But I cannot let Malathy go."

Maya brushed away the tears that sprang from recalling these painful events. She pulled down what she could, feeling far more pain in the loss of the little objects that she and Rahul had picked up on various trips, than the massive solid oak furniture pieces that the interior designer had selected for the room. Every little object in the room seemed to have a memory, a shared history of their years together. Tears flowing freely, Maya carefully wrapped each piece and placed it in a box, the snapping sound of thick sticky tape, sealing each possession. The memories refused to be sealed away.

15

THE CLOSEST TO HOME

As much as she had detested their crass ways all her life, Maya yearned for that sense of simplicity, that ordinariness as never before. As her social circles in the Capital buzzed with the news of the break-down of her high profile marriage, she wanted to take the train to the nondescript small town, which her father had once called home. She yearned to place her tired face in the folds of a crumpled and bright nylon sari (just the kind of gaudy, wholesale print she had detested all her life). She wanted so much to sit on a not-so-comfortable (but so practical) metal chair gazing through a window adorned with cheap, washable, un-coordinated curtains.

When Maya called Bua to say she'd be visiting, Bua was ecstatic, "*Beti*, tell *Jamai Raja chawal ki kheer* will be waiting. He still likes it doesn't he? Make sure you are here in time for lunch and no need to send the driver away somewhere else. Let him eat here."

Maya had not visited her for years, in fact she had barely bothered to keep in touch and Bua had no idea about the upheavals in her life. "Bua, I am coming alone by train. I'll take an auto home don't worry. Rahul, I don't think he will be able to join me, no not even after a few days Bua. But I'm coming,"

Maya hung up. After Rahul realized it was impossible to stop Maya from walking out, he had been angry, very very angry. Maya had been crying all night, yet another night, as she packed to leave. Despite his wrath, there was no nastiness. Numbed by the finality of her own decision, Maya, for the first time in her life, did not care for money. Besides, what would she do with all that she had? In good old Pathankot, nobody would notice the softness of the leather of her designer handbag or whether her shoes displayed the subtle but sure high profile brand. Still, she packed fifteen suitcases full of all her fancy clothes, an enviable range of shoes, cosmetics, and jewellery…everything. She was going for good and she wanted to leave no traces of her physical self behind. Preeti, who had stood by Maya through all this, never offering comment or unsolicited advice, had offered to keep all of Maya's stuff until she decided what she wanted to do with her life. When Preeti's driver and Man Friday arrived to pick up all her stuff, Maya had the cases neatly lined up in the spacious lobby of her sprawling home.

For just that half-hour, while the duo swiftly loaded the cases into Preeti's huge multi-utility vehicle, Maya maintained her usual poise, her pencil heels clicking across the marble floor as she issued instructions, never offering to even lift a vanity case herself. Minutes after the duo left, she burst into tears again.

16

JUST LIKE THE MOVIES

Maya had not been to Pathankot for years. It had been even longer since she undertook a journey by the great Indian railways. A few years ago, Maya and Rahul had enjoyed the lavish and sanitized experience of a 'Palace on Wheels' vacation along with an Australian couple they knew from one of Rahul's brief overseas stints. And that journey in the lap of luxury would hardly have prepared Maya for this one from Delhi to Pathankot. Despite the "AC two-tier" ticket that she had booked herself in, Maya spent the night tossing in her cushioned but narrow railway berth. The coffee was unbearably sweet with milk powder floating on top (for years now, Maya had lived on sugarless Cappuccino) and the worst of all- the toilets stank.

When Maya alighted at Chakki Bank railway station (Bua had told her she would find it easier to get a rickshaw at Chakki bank than at Pathankot station though the latter was closer) the next morning, she was bleary eyed and yearning for a hot shower. Despite her physical exhaustion, Maya had not lost hope. As she waited outside the wooden shed that made for a railway ticket office, Maya's eyes searched not for auto-rickshaw drivers but Rahul's familiar face. It had happened in numerous mushy novels that Maya had devoured, in all the predictable movies she had endured, the hero always returned to the arms of his heroine. She thought of Rahul speeding through rugged terrain in his BMW to get to Pathankot before she did or even hiring a helicopter to prove to her how repentant he was. She thought of him waiting there with a bouquet of her favourite white roses, just like he had after their first fight years ago. For 45 minutes, Maya stood there, and Rahul did not come.

The nip in the early morning air was gone and the chirping birds were replaced by the honking of auto-rickshaw drivers. The tears just would not stop. She kneeled down as if to adjust the strap of her sandals and gently dabbed her eyes with her soft linen scarf before she rose. She hailed an auto rickshaw and made her way to Bua's old home.

It was in that house with inexpensive but functional furniture and an aunt who had withered in the same floral printed nylon sari that Maya found recluse. The edges of Bua's mouth had puckered in, the dentures (sponsored by Suketu and his wife Jyoti in the US) didn't fit as well as they should have. There was also a new 29-inch flat-screen television in Bua's otherwise dingy drawing room- Suketu's doing no doubt. Or more likely, Jyoti's.

Years ago, when Maya had met Jyoti for the first time at the Delhi airport when Suketu and Jyoti were due to fly out to the US, Jyoti's demeanor had oozed the aura of old money. Jyoti certainly added a unique and diametrically opposite dimension to the family that Maya had been embarrassed to be seen with.

Maya could just imagine the pride her Dad would have felt in having a next of kin NRI— his own sister's son and his wife living in the US! The United States of America mind you, not obscure destinations in the Middle East where even Hindu Indian women had to cover their faces and where Sunayana's siblings had chosen to spend most of their lives- all for the money. Magical. America offered the "quality of life" that Maya's father had valued so much all his life.

Bua had hot water running for her and breakfast of crispy gobi paranthas with dollops of white homemade butter. Maya had not touched butter for years to maintain her washboard stomach. Too weak to stand up to Bua's coaxing, Maya ate well and gladly sank into the razai clutching the hot water bottle Bua had thoughtfully placed there an hour earlier.

For days after that, Maya slept and slept, getting up to eat the sumptuous meals that Bua placed before her. In the evenings she walked alone, visiting the spots she and her Dad frequented during her summer holidays with Bua.

During one of her walks back home from her favourite Dad spots, Maya offered to do some grocery shopping for Bua. Compared to the elaborate lists that Maya always armed herself with, Bua's list had just five items and nothing exotic at all. Even Maya's trained staff had words like broccoli, jalapenos, and cheddar cheese rolling off their tongues easily. Under Maya's eagle eye, they were trained enough to hold their own in a five-star setting. And fair enough, after Maya's departure from home, one of them had bagged an assignment as hospitality in-charge in a large corporate house.

Well, Bua's list would have been far too infra-dig by Maya's standards, but here in Pathankot and given her state of mind, she did not care. In fact, as she stepped into the cluttered grocery shop where dusty glass bottles of aerated soft drinks jostled for space with stuffed, sun-dried chillis, she actually found herself picking up a few more things for Bua.

Maya was clad in one of her simplest salwar kmeez outfits teamed with near-flat heeled sandals. But the touch of class Maya had yearned for during the better part of her existence refused to go. As Maya's refined voice uttered the contents of Bua's grocery list, all other activity seemed to come to a standstill. The shop owner too thought it an occasion enough to merit slipping off his massive backside from the stool behind the counter and offer his undivided attention to Maya. Of course, what he essentially did was repeat Maya's utterances in a much louder voice with a comment or two of his own.

"Basmati rice!" he would holler adding, "Chotu, get the packet from the shelf in the inner room. Madam must have the best!" His cronies, (on red alert considering the importance of the occasion—the master himself had stepped off his stool!) scrambled to get what Madam wanted. As the other customers

Just Like the Movies

waited reverently, Maya stepped out of the modest grocery establishment, shopping bag packed to the brim, a trifle embarrassed and amused as well.

Maya's finishing school style workshop trainer would have been proud of the effect Maya was generating, even though it was just in a small town grocery shop setting. Maya's carefully manicured hands, her shoulder-length immaculately styled streaked brown hair and more-over, the elegant gait and modulated voice she had acquired over years of 'finishing school interventions' and self-training, just refused to go.

As she walked back to Bua's house, she thought back at her decision to enroll into a finishing school. It was in the sixth year of their marriage and Rahul's salary was now good enough for Maya to be able to quit her unsatisfying job. Her premise was that upper class women did not work for anyone else, they either ran boutiques set up by their husbands and conned other rich wives into buying their over-priced ware, or else, were involved in highly visible socially useful and productive roles.

By then, Rahul was also doing well enough to buy their second car. Maya not only chucked her job, but promptly recruited a chauffeur for the new acquisition… yet another premise she lived by—"Upper class women did not use their cars like pick-up trucks, stuffing them with groceries and house-hold stuff. More-over, they did not spend a better part of their lives stressing themselves out in navigating traffic or trying to jostle for parking space in over-crowded markets. Upper class women also displayed a high level of dependence mostly on their husbands. And when the husband was fashionably "traveling", were driven around by their personal chauffeurs."

Rahul had no idea about Maya's premise and thought Maya was perfectly capable of learning to drive. But when Maya repeatedly expressed this inexplicable terror of driving, he reluctantly let the chauffer into their lives. And whenever the chauffer did not turn up, Maya, with her obsession with fitness, walked. So walking in Pathankot was no big change.

Bua asked her if Rahul was out of the country. Maya just nodded.

"Then this is the time to enjoy yourself in your *mayka* (parental home)," she smiled, patting Maya's hand.

At the mention of the term 'parental' Maya winced, but simply did not have the emotional energy to relate all that had happened, not now, maybe later.

At this moment and for years to come, Maya was consumed by the thought of what she did wrong for Rahul to drift away. What was it that Rahul had seen in her years ago that had been lost? Had she not tried hard enough?

17

BEAUTY AND THE BEHOLDER

There was a part of Rahul, which probably even he did not know or want to acknowledge- that was unmistakably traditional Indian male. Deep in his mind, his idea of a sensual woman was one with a buxom, filled-out body. However, through their marital relationship he had encouraged Maya in her pursuit to be like the global image of beauty – reed thin, immaculately made-up on all occasions and dressed in the latest Western styles.

Maya, intent on being the best turned out among the celebrity wives' circuit and of course believing earnestly that her aim for a super model like figure was shared by her husband, had pulled out all stops. Lipo-suction for the thighs, tummy tucks, bust line correction, hip-line correction, and electrolysis for the stray strands of hair between her eyebrows… Maya had been there and done all of that. As she graduated from grimy "residence cum beauty parlors" run by homemakers, to the exorbitantly priced, swanky beauty spas in Delhi's five-star hotels, Maya found herself slowly getting sucked into the whirlpool of beautician induced need for "treatments".

Maya took great pride in her reed-thin, super-model like body. At an age when the slimmest of women usually begin to show a little weight around the hips, Maya could afford to breeze into any trendy boutique and blithely slip into a slinky blouse or a pair of trousers designed for women less than half her age. There were others like her in the "wives" circuit who took their children out for a swim at the five-star club instead of pigging out at fast-food eateries. It was these women who guzzled 0% skimmed milk in imported tetra cans instead of patronizing the buxom buffalos of India, who inspired Maya to stick to her rigorous diet regime. Despite the trim body, in her pursuit of this dashboard stomach, Maya had lost that healthy glow, the full-bodied and completely natural look that she had when she and Rahul first met years ago.

But Maya also encountered the likes of Charu Batra, who most certainly would prefer to order (and given her diamond spangled persona may even be served) a channa bhatura or paneer makhanwala in a specialty Thai or Italian restaurant. With a hearty pat on her ample bosom, Charu would wave her plump arms at Maya proclaiming, *"Yeh sub diet shiet hum se nahi hoga. Ghar mein bache hain."* (I can't handle these diets of yours. After all, I have kids at home). The kitchen has got to be stocked with potato chips, colas, burgers and ice cream. Maya would cringe at the poorly disguised reference to her "childlessness".

In the early days, such jabs would instantly bring tears to Maya's eyes until Rahul taught her to deal with the likes of Charu Batra. But Maya knew she had been lucky. In the middle-class society that she had grown up in, her "childless state" would have attracted curiosity and comment to a far greater degree. She could not imagine living her life among the queries of well-meaning distant aunts, nosy neighbours and casual acquaintances. In the circles that Maya now moved in, people by no means, were less nosy or devoid of gossip. But not being asked about one's marital status or motherhood, at least not till you got to know someone well, was a norm borrowed from the Westernized society they all liked to believe they belonged to. Despite the years that had passed by, the pain of not having a child was still real.

18

PRIORITIES

Maya was working in the same law firm, now at a slightly elevated position, her monthly salary up from Rs. 6000 to Rs. 10,000 when she discovered she was pregnant. For any other married woman in Maya's position, the news of pregnancy would have been a source of joy. Even Rahul, if he had found out earlier, would have been thrilled once the initial shock and the financial burden it would bring, had waned. But Rahul never found out, Maya never told him, until it was far too late.

Maya was ten weeks pregnant when that liquid in the home-pregnancy test turned pale pink instead of the dark pink she had hope it would. She had finally mustered the courage to take the test. She told herself she didn't want the baby - Rahul just could not afford any breaks at this point in his career. Maya knew (for she managed the finances, whatever little it came to at the end of each month), that Rahul's Executive Masters Programme in Singapore would mean hoarding every spare penny of her Rs.10,000/- salary.

Rahul was away when Maya found out she was expecting. In any case, Maya had absolutely no intention of telling him. She was determined he would have no distractions however temporary. After all, their future depended

Maya

on Rahul's MBA, As of now, the scholarship was for his tuition alone. His air-fare and living expenses had to be borne by them –at least till he found himself a part-time job. And if Maya had a baby, she would lose this law-firm job. She was on this strange and unfair "contract" policy which allowed no maternity benefits, and they simply could not afford to sacrifice his University admission for that.

Having told herself that she was just in her twenties and had more than two decades of child-bearing years before her, Maya set out to visit a gynaecologist. Instead of her usual gynaecologist at a nearby co-operative hospital, (lest the well-meaning lady tried to talk her out of the decision or insisted that Rahul talk to her) Maya went to the biggest and most expensive corporate hospital in New Delhi. She had heard too many horror stories about the Rs.199/- only sleazy abortion clinics in the poorer congested part of New Delhi.

Sensibly reflecting that her health was more than worth the Rs. 5000/- she would spend on the minor 'procedure' at the Sunbeams hospital, Maya walked across the granite flooring in the opulent hospital lobby. Dr. Khurana was away, she was told by the prim painted lady at the Sunbeams reception, would she like to see the junior Dr. Khurana instead (the Grand Old Man's son) who had just joined his father's noble profession?

Maya hesitated. She wanted experienced hands handling her delicate condition, not blue blood!

"No I'd like a meeting with Dr. Khurana senior please, whenever that is possible-actually at the earliest, I want to go in for an abortion," Maya blurted, beads of perspiration on her forehead.

The prim lady, who had obviously taken in Maya's imitation handbag and simple but elegant cotton salwar kameez outfit with disdain, became even more patronizing.

"Dear, the senior doc is away in the States to attend an international conference. He will not return for another three weeks. But if you could pay the booking charges right away, I could give you an appointment directly for an MTP (Medical Termination of Pregnancy) on January the 15th. As the lady tapped the pencil on her desk, Maya saw that the date was a good three weeks away, but still reasoned that a consultation with the senior doctor was worth the wait.

"That will be Rs.1500/- please Miss_____ ?", Ms Prim Painted raised an eyebrow.

"Mrs. Sikand - Maya Rahul Sikand" said Maya, a little too loudly, counting out thirty Rs.50 notes to hand them over as her hand unconsciously touched the bright red spot of sindhoor at the edge of her hairline, clearly proclaiming her marital status.

"Oh that's fine my dear," purred Ms. Prim Painted with a look that said, "They all say that, I've heard that one before! Where's the chap who got you into this mess anyway."

When Maya presented herself before Ms Prim Painted three weeks later, she was handed an official-looking declaration form, "The name and phone number of your husband or next of kin please-in case of an emergency."

"Er, my husband is traveling; there is no-one else. I'm sure I'll be fine", Maya smiled bravely. This time Ms PP almost jeered as if, to say,

"Been having a little bit of fun behind the hubby's back and your boyfriend ditched you too sweetie or do you have a husband in the first place?"

She uttered none of these, but simply ushered Maya into Dr. Khurana's inner chambers. Changed into a pale blue hospital gown, Maya was made to lie down and spread her legs wide. A nurse walked in and deftly fastened her feet into stirrups. A young lady doctor noted down her medical history-her last missed period, age, was she allergic to anything, and was she aware of the risks involved in the MTP procedure. Tense and scared, Maya nodded mutely and put her signature on yet another declaration form.

Minutes later, the expert hands she had waited three weeks for, were examining her.

Maya

Discarding his disposable gloves after the internal examination, Dr. Khurana crisply uttered complex medical abbreviations that Maya could not understand. The nurse noted down Dr. Khurana's instructions and Maya was whisked to the operation theatre unaware that the events of the next half hour would change her life forever. Maya closed her eyes, letting herself drift into the anaesthesia induced slumber, looking forward to being told she was not "expecting any more" when she would regain consciousness a few hours later.

But Maya did not regain consciousness for the next 24 hours. And when she did, there was a sharp pain searing through her lower abdomen and thighs as she lay in a dimly lit room, a pale blue curtain separating her frail body from another hospital bed. Lying on the other side was the frail form of Preeti, the daughter-in-law of the city's illustrious Mitra family, in the intensive care unit of the city's premium hospital.

As Maya cried out in pain, a portly form in a nurse's uniform walked up to her bedside and injected a creamy fluid into the plastic bottle of intra-venous fluid dangling by her bedside. She placed her large, rough palm gently on Maya's forehead whispering,

"You need to rest Maya. There has been so much blood loss. Only rest and good care will help you get your strength back." Maya slipped back into a deep, drug-induced sleep.

"Sister!" it was Preeti from the other bed.

"Yes Mrs. Mitra, how can I help?" the nurse walked up to Preeti respectfully. Preeti, now at the brink of being moved out of the ICU and into her own deluxe room in the hospital, sat up.

"Oh I don't need anything Sister. You always have everything in place and take such good care of everyone. And you know, if it had not been for my husband worrying so much, I would have been in the private room days ago and probably home by now!" said Preeti with a wan smile.

The nurse smiled back warmly.

Priorities

"Oh the dear young man and such a loving husband! You know Mrs. Mitra, your husband was born in this hospital. I was very much here. Your mother-in-law is one tough lady, bearing everything with such courage. I remember so clearly. She came into the hospital in labour, happily married with sindoor on her forehead and jangling bangles. Your husband was born healthy alright but then, two days after, when she was waiting for the child's father to come and see his first-born, she got the shocking news of his death in the air-crash. The lady hugged the baby and wept for days, but only when no-one was around. When she left the hospital with the boy in her arms 10 days later, she walked out in her white sari, sindhoor washed away, but no tears, just determination in her step," the nurse smiled at the memory.

Preeti of course had heard this story and many others of her mother-in-law's courage...stories of how she brushed away oily cousins of her husband who seemed to crawl out of the woodwork after his untimely death, ostensibly to "help" her manage his widespread business interests. Refusing to sign any of the documents they produced, she went on to seek counsel from a handful of her husband's trusted employees and walked into her husband's office 25 days after her husband's death and after she became a mother. What she did not know, she would ask and what others could not or would not tell her, she would plunge in, experience herself, fall and learn as she picked herself up again! Preeti was used to meeting the Grand Old Lady's admirers. And Sister Marium here was clearly one of them!

"Sister, actually I was wondering what's wrong with the lady across there. There's been no-one to visit her and she obviously seems to be in great pain. Is there something we can do to help her?" asked Preeti.

Though kind-hearted, Sister Mariam had been waiting to share her concerns about this particular patient with someone. She considered the giggly trainee nurses she had been saddled with, far below her stature to discuss anything like this with. Sister Mariam had to even ask them to pin their hair properly under the nurse's cap and insist their uniforms were well below the knee. Did they teach nothing at nursing school these days? Familiarity with these flighty ones was out of question!

Maya

Sister Mariam quickly decided that the younger Mrs. Mitra was just the person to speak to about this. She related all that she knew about Maya's tragic experience to Preeti.

"Checked in all by herself for an abortion saying her husband is travelling. Seems to be from a good, educated, middle-class family. Probably is afraid of what her parents would do if they found out. Poor child. It's God's will," sighed Sister Mariam, touching the metal chain and cross that rested on her ample chest.

What Sister Mariam did not know, and thus did not say, was this:

By insisting on waiting to see the senior Dr. Khurana only, Maya was already over the 12-week safe period when she had her abortion. After examining her, the senior Dr. Khurana had received an emergency call and had to rush to the airport. Among the senior doctor's illustrious patients were wives of Sultans and oil-rich Sheikhs in the UAE, film stars and celebrities, willing to shell out absolutely any price for the good doctor's magical touch. One such private jet had landed at Delhi airport waiting to transport him straight to the palace. The payment for this VIP service (in cash and gold bars) had arrived by the same jet and was safely ensconced in his home.

The senior doctor would rather have finished the procedure at hand and then left, but there had been a call from Dubai already politely urging him to leave within minutes, the car was waiting.

Dr. Khurana did not miss the sinister undercurrent in that polite call. The payment has been made and the service is overdue. The debt of the past few years had taken its toll on the good doctor – the state of the art medical equipment upgrades, the refurbishing of the deluxe floor with five star facilities and most of all, financing his son's medical education in Russia. The best coaching classes and international schooling seemed to have had no impact on his only son's dismal academic performance. Even private medical colleges across India refused to admit him. Sending him to Russia was the only choice if the hospital of his dreams was to continue running. With piling debt and patients who owned his time, Dr. Khurana knew he had lost the choice to do what was morally right. Dr. Khurana rushed out of the hospital to catch his flight telling his personal assistant to reschedule the procedure for two days later when he would certainly be back.

But with his father out of the way and the patient already under anaesthesia, the young Dr. Khurana strode into the operation theatre. With supreme confidence and the arrogance of defying his father and one of the many patients who still requested to only be treated by his father and not him, he declared that he would be performing the procedure – it was a routine one after all.

The attending operation theatre staff and even the young doctor were never to forget the frenzy of the next two hours… the bloodbath of Maya's overgrown foetus and the ripping of her uterine wall, the hasty patch-up job to contain the flow of blood, the panic of the dangerous drop in her blood pressure…

When Rahul eventually found out, he did not weep, he did not speak either. He was too overwhelmed by it all, rudely shaken out of his jet lag by the tragic circumstances he had returned to. Time they say heals everything. But in this case, the pain of having lost a baby that they could never again have was too raw, for Maya and for Rahul as well. But he did not blame Maya. The trauma she had been through and the very fact that she had decided to take this risk and brave it all alone—the fact that she did it for his professional growth, however misplaced that sentiment may be, did not escape him either. A part of Rahul was deeply touched by this. Another tiny corner of him (which was to surface much later), was hardened by the knowledge that Maya could do anything for his and her own socio- economic escalation.

But despite the love for children that both of them shared, Rahul never warmed up to the idea of adoption. A few years after the tragedy, when the Sikands were finally ensconced in their sprawling home, Maya broached the topic of bringing home a baby. Rahul did not refuse straight away, taking refuge in eternal film-script favourites like.

"Why do we need a third person to intrude on this life-long honeymoon?" and,

Maya

"You've got me to pamper and I've got you sweetheart!"

Maya persisted, subtly at first. Exasperated with his procrastination and her craving for motherhood growing with the continuous torture of having to attend elaborate baby showers at affluent venues, Maya finally had Rahul confess that the idea of adoption did not appeal to him at all. He could not bring himself to put down the reason but Maya persisted,

"Are you worried about the child's lineage?" she asked. Rahul shook his head.

"Are you worried that the child might have a genetic disorder? If our child had one, would we not accept whatever it was?" asked Maya desperately.

"I don't know if I will be able to love anyone else's child the same way. And if I don't, it would not be fair to the child," said Rahul quietly. Slipping into her "good wife who does not nag like Sunayana" role all over again, Maya never mentioned adoption ever again. Had she done so, it would have probably been better for both of them.

19

SUPER MUM

For years later, when Rahul accompanied Malathy and her two boys for a swim and lunch, he felt a strange surge of affection towards the young ones. Maybe Malathy's manner of handling them made it seem easy. She tackled their queries with confidence, never afraid to answer any difficult question, prying them away from screechy virtual warfare and prodding them into outdoor activities. It appeared to Rahul that Malathy had done a wonderful job of ensuring that the prolonged absence of their father did not make them grow up as sissies. As he watched the two boys romp about, Rahul felt a growing confidence that he wanted the three of them, Malathy and the two young Turks in his life, forever.

But Malathy was certain she did not want to complicate her children's lives with such ideas in what she considered, was a nascent stage of their relationship. In her organized mind, time with the children and time with Rahul came under separate heads and rarely did she let them overlap, and today was an exception.

Though she and Rahul had been living together for three months now, this was the first time she had included the children in their plans. Even then, she made sure she picked them up from tennis lessons in her own car and asked Rahul to meet them at the pool. Wrapped up in each other and thrilled to see their mother after three days, they accepted Rahul as Mum's friend and colleague without a second thought.

For over a decade now, Malathy had accepted the loneliness of her long distance marriage as a small price to pay for the "security" her husband's job offered and more important, the understanding and love they shared. The growing proximity to Rahul had made her question why she should stay in a marriage with a man who may be loved her, or may be he didn't. One could pretend for three months a year, if it bought peace for the rest of the nine months. Malathy was questioning whether her husband had the right to resent her job (which gave her deep satisfaction and had sustained her intellectual well-being for years) during the few months that he was here. For the first time, Malathy had dared to think of a future for herself and Rahul and much to her surprise, Rahul had not ruled out the possibility.

Malathy's brain, used to sorting out logistics in quick and often ingenious ways, had it all figured out in just a few days. Her kids would move in with Amma and Appa, at least for the time being. She would explain to the older one that she was doing a "residential workshop", which required her to be at work night and day and that she'd visit them every two days and try and spend at least two nights a week with them.

Her younger child, she knew, would repeat what the older one said and that too with conviction so that even Amma and her gossipy friends in the neighbourhood would believe the story. As of now, Malathy thought it best not to upset the applecart and cause grief to her parents. Her husband, when he called, would not even ask what workshop this was.

It was strange the way Pradeep was so possessive when he was with her and near indifferent and pre-occupied when he was away. Telephone conversations usually revolved around updates on the children's progress at school, the younger one's antics and his prowess at the swimming pool or the older one's wise cracks that revealed a level of maturity beyond his seven years. Pradeep rarely asked Malathy about her work or what she did with her long, active (with swimming, lunches and movies for the children) but lonely weekends. Malathy didn't know what Pradeep did with his leisure time either or what his work involved on a day to day basis. She would have loved to know and be the emotional crutch she truly believed each human being needed, especially during difficult times.

After the boisterous swim and lunch, later in the evening, after Malathy had picked up new school shoes for the duo, their favorite snacks for a school outing the next day and assembled the props for a class project, Malathy and Rahul were alone in their pad again.

He on his laptop, she on hers. There were 84 e-mails to answer, 26 on which Rahul had been copied (just to be kept in the loop) by managers at various levels in the company. And this after Rahul had checked his e-mail just 5 hours ago. But the intense concentration that Maya admired in him and yet wished she could invade, seemed to have disappeared. Rahul quickly scanned the unread mail list to see whether there was something that could not wait till next morning. To his surprise, there wasn't. He shut down the device and put it away. In yet another move that would have startled Maya, he brewed some masala chai and walked over to Malathy with two steaming mugs. Malathy was dressed in a simple loose fitting cotton kaftan (unlike the finely crafted slinky satin two/three piece night suits that Maya used), her long dark hair in an untidy knot, held in place with, well… right now it seemed to be like a ballpoint pen! Even in her simplicity and her natural Indian woman figure, to Rahul, she looked beautiful.

The days had flown past as they spent every waking moment together. What was it about Maya and what was it about Malathy? That Maya did her very best for Rahul and more and Malathy simply let him be?

20

MAKING PEACE

The way Maya hated to answer queries about why she and Rahul had no children, she would cringe every time someone would inquire about her *mayka* (parental home). Technically, Maya did not have a *mayka* home as such. For all these years, she had not treated Bua as anything but a distant relative, maintaining minimal contact and never really bothering to visit much. Years had gone by since Sunayana's death and the dismantling of her parental home. Today, when she did not have her own home to speak of, Maya finally allowed herself to be irked by the man she hated the most in the world — her father. For years, she had been determined in her refusal to let any memories of him to disturb her. Now she wanted to confront them all.

Having healed her body with the quiet comfort that Bua offered her, Maya bid farewell to her old aunt. She promised to visit soon and just nodded when Bua insisted that she bring Rahul along the next time.

Maya arrived in dusty Agra to be assaulted by greedy touts on the lookout for rich tourists. Though the idea of an Indian woman holidaying alone in North India was uncommon, Maya had the moneyed look that put her almost on par with the white-skinned tourists that flocked to visit the Taj Mahal. Maya

Making Peace

brushed aside youngsters selling picture postcards of the Taj and Agra Fort and hailed an auto-rickshaw.

"I take you very good hotel Madam, hop, jump and Taj Mahal, beautiful, beautiful Taj view!" gushed the auto-rickshaw driver grinning at Maya. Maya briskly informed him that she did not want to see the Taj and that he should take her to the mental asylum.

"Aha research type! Is your camera and crew expected too once you check things out? Let me know, I can make arrangements for everyone's stay. *Haanji,*" the driver exclaimed with the air of one who has seen it all. Convinced that Maya was a representative of a rich non-governmental organization (NGO) or a documentary film maker, he continued with a toothy grin,

"Madamji, *in paagalon ka kuch nahin hone wala* (There is nothing to be done with these mad hatters). Once they get into the asylum, there is only one way out," he pointed upwards. Maya grabbed her suitcase to jump out of the auto-rickshaw when the vehicle sputtered into motion, the over smart driver muttering, "OK OK, no offence, I'll take you to the asylum. To each his own..."

Maya met the medical officer on duty, filled out a lengthy form detailing the reason for her visit, her relationship with the patient and a declaration that she would leave all electronic gadgets, money and other valuables outside before she stepped into the enclosure for patients. With a worn-out cardboard visitor's card in her sweaty palm, Maya began the long walk to meet patient number 187.

Years of living in a rented apartment had ensured that his name was never prominently displayed on the door of their home, and now, this number for an identity.

He had no special talent, he never worked with passion, but all his life, he strove to be a good father and he loved Maya unconditionally. As a child, she had responded to his tenderness, easily drawn to him by the fact that he made time for her, that when he played with her, he would offer his undivided attention. This was in sharp contrast with Sunayana's brusque efficiency and her struggle to acquire material comforts for her small family. Sunayana too loved Maya deeply but she never did have the patience to pause and listen to what her only child ever had to say.

As Maya stepped into adolescence, she veered toward her mother, conditioned by Sunayana's continuous exhortation of how her father could have done much better in life if only he had been more enterprising. In Maya's impressionable young mind, Sunayana loomed larger than life, as the woman who did it all and had been cheated in life by a marriage to this "ordinary" and as Sunayana often said, "lazy" man.

Maya's father was not lazy. Among the neatly arranged tables in his office, his table was always the cleanest. Despite Sunayana's vociferous nagging every morning, he was always at work at the dot of ten and stayed away from the bunch of colleagues who spent a sizable chunk of time sipping tea in the canteen.

Maya's father was the first to be offered the Voluntary Retirement Scheme (VRS) package when the bank underwent a massive digitalization exercise, not because he was inefficient, or lazy, but simply because he had no Godfather to protect his interests and the management knew that he would not protest or approach the Staff Unions.

If he had been 'well-connected', he would have found a friend who knew someone with an Uncle in the right political circles to stall the forced retirement order.

If he had been aggressive, he would have questioned the digitalization and why new 'IT-trained' staff was being recruited while loyal and efficient employees like him were being retrenched.

If he had been pro-active, he would have suggested to the management that he and others like him be offered the training in using the new IT-based packages. If he could think out of the box, he would have approached one of the multitudes of IT-training outlets in the city and invested in a basic IT

Making Peace

training course himself. It did not cost all that much and for someone like him used to dealing with numbers and precisely following a set of instructions, he would have mastered it in weeks.

He was none of these. He quietly signed on the dotted line, smiled graciously during the speech his manager made at the 'Send-off' gathering organized for him, nibbled at the single samosa and potato chips laid out on a paper-plate and appeared grateful to be presented a wall-clock imprinted with the bank's logo as a token of appreciation for his decades of service.

"Enjoy your retirement. And come and see us some time!" his colleagues bid him farewell and went back to clearing their dusty desks. The shiny white computers were to arrive very soon and the paper files had to make way for these new entrants.

The series of managers he had worked for during his tenure at the bank, would certainly describe him as diligent and dependable, provided they managed to recall his name. For Maya's father could easily blend into a crowd or even be dismissed as inconsequential and he did not mind. But Sunayana did. Frustrated at her inability to change the man she had married, she ceaselessly needled him all her life, hurtling stray insults at his simplicity, in private and yes, in public as well.

Maya's father had borne the humiliation in silence, further withdrawing into his shell every time Sunayana insulted him in public… until the night of terror years ago.

21

SILENCE

Maya was led down the corridor and into an open courtyard. Suddenly, she was overcome by the irrepressible urge to back out and run away.

"Number 187, someone to see you!" the attendant announced gruffly and walked away instructing Maya to deposit the visitor's card at the reception window on her way out. Maya lowered her head, her sweaty palm clutching the cardboard number tag, petrified to look up.

"Excuse me Madam." A gnarled brown hand gently touched Maya's elbow. The voice belonged to an inmate of the hospital dressed in the dull grey cotton shirt and ankle length pyjamas that Maya had seen others wearing as she walked along the corridors.

"I'm Kulwant Singh. To this asylum of course, I am Number 156. Don't be afraid, I won't harm you. Of course, the court has pronounced me insane and spared me a death sentence. I killed my daughter's rapist in a fit of rage. Whether that brute deserved to die, of course he did. Whether I had the right to kill him, may be as a civilized citizen of the country, I didn't. As a father haunted by his daughter's heart wrenching screams, maybe I did," he said, clearly willing to talk to anyone who was willing to listen.

Silence

Shocked, Maya stared hard at the steel gray eyes under the gray turban and the jaw set in determination partially covered by the flowing gray beard.

"I'm here to see... er Number 187," she mumbled.

"Oh, no documentary film then, no chance to get famous in my old age!" Kulwant Singh gave her a wry smile, motioning her to follow him as he ambled across the courtyard, continuing to talk.

"Now number 187, that story has enigma! Whether he is insane or was just pronounced insane, no one knows. He does not harm anyone. He does not speak. No one knows his name; it must be buried in the dusty files somewhere. He follows instructions, bathes, shaves, eats what is given to him, even does the weaving or sorting or whatever work they assign him, but mostly sits under the peepal tree out there, staring into thin air. They say he is educated; he used to work in a bank. May be he lost his head for numbers with old age, that is possible. But what I find impossible to believe is that a timid soul like him is a murderer and he killed his own wife!"

"Babu, Madam has come to see you, at least look at her," Kulwant Singh bent down to tap on the shoulder of a thin figure seated under the peepal tree.

Shrunk into a shadow of his erstwhile enthusiastic self, Maya could barely recognize him. As she looked into his sunken eyes, he gave her a long blank stare. Was there barely a flicker of recognition that she missed before his eyes settled into nothingness?

There was no drama, no tearful embrace, and no attempt to recapture the years that had slipped by.

His gaunt form had said nothing, but Maya had finally confronted the ghosts of the past— of the hate for her parents she had lived with, hating her mother for the years of humiliation that she had subjected her father to and hating her father for enduring it in silence, finally leading to the fatal assault.

Maya

Clearly he was in a world of his own, lost in a guilt ridden existence, never forgiving himself for the death of the woman he loved and hated so much.

It was too late. Maya could do nothing but move on...

22

CORPORATE HEALING

Having made peace with what was left of her roots, Maya thought it was time to move on and seek peace within herself.

Preeti had mentioned a 'Self discovery through active meditation' programme that her husband Sushanto had implemented for 'Vice-Presidents and above and their spouses' in his company. Preeti too had tagged along with Sushanto for this weekend affair. Her purpose was clear:

1. So that Sushanto would be able to set a good example by attending the programme he had recommended and dedicated a sizable budget for.

2. To steal at least a few moments of quality time with Sushanto without the kids and the looming presence of her dominating ma-in-law.

With her string of heirloom pearls, carefully styled crop of pepper-grey hair and chiffon or finely spun cotton saris in pastel shades, the senior Mrs. Mitra was a force to reckon with and highly respected among corporate circles. Having ruled her husband's group of companies with an iron fist after his premature death, senior Mrs. Mitra applied the iron hand mechanism to her only son Sushanto and his family as well. She had fixed notions about what Preeti and her children should and should not do with themselves and was forever goading them into what she saw as constructive and culturally enriching pursuits. At 71, Mrs. Mitra's energy and zest for life certainly surpassed that of Preeti and her two adorable, but rather shy children. Preeti's own illustrious family origins had resulted in the well-approved Sushanto-Preeti arranged match. Preeti being a devoted wife and mother, there really was no reason for any mother-in-law to have any complaints about her. But senior Mrs. Mitra expected spunk and ambition in everyone around her so Preeti appeared 'insipid' to her on this count.

Maya was a frequent visitor at the Mitra household. Despite Maya's attempts to curtail her personal ambition, her spunk shone through. Maya and Mrs. Mitra shared an amicable relationship.

Sushanto had ensured that his mother had not been able to wheedle her way into attending the first workshop he and Preeti had been part of. The success of the first workshop for 'VPs and above' had led to the organizing of a second session for the company's board of advisors and select top management that had missed out on session 1. Naturally, Mrs. Mitra was attending and on Preeti's request, a slot was reserved for Maya and Maya agreed to tag along.

At the picturesque seven-star resort in Bharatpur, Maya had been placed into the lap of nature to help her heal herself. Blindfolded walks in pairs to "help one actualize the potential of the other senses, especially the touch", a high tech cleansing diet for a day followed by a candid session on "What I wish my neighbour did not have but I did"… the workshop was a true corporatised, customized attempt at "detoxifying stressed out souls" at the company's cost. Maya went through the motions of openly absorbing positive thoughts from the enthusiastic trainer only half listening. Meanwhile, Mrs. M was nodding wisely, snapping her manicured fingers at punch lines, jotting down a particularly inspiring thought. In spite of the trainer's enthusiastic attempts to "transmit positive thoughts by absorption", Maya's

Corporate Healing

mind refused to be pulled away from the painful memories of the recent past. Her thoughts flitted from the sight of her father's gaunt figure to Rahul's stony silence when she asked him whether Malathy's recent appearance in his life nullified her years of unquestionable devotion to their marriage.

After the last inspiring session, all the participants were blindfolded and were asked to sit still for 15 minutes listening to soothing music.

"When the music stops, you must let go of yourself and let the predominant emotion in you gush forth – laughter, shouting, dancing, clapping, singing, stamping your feet… however you best wish to express how you now feel. Do what you really want to do and do not hold back on account of your business suits," exhorted the trainer before slipping into a quiet corner to switch on soothing music.

When the music stopped, the room erupted into a cacophony of yells, screeches, thumps, claps and uninhibited guffaws.

Maya only sank to the floor and wept.

23

MRS. NO-ONE

"Why do you want to adopt a child Mrs. Sikand," asked the government representative peering above the dog-eared paper files on his dusty desk. Maya flinched at the use of Rahul's surname to address her. She had lived with Rahul's surname for all her adult life.

"If anyone at all, Malathy should be using Rahul's second name," thought Maya wryly. Not that she liked the use of her father's second name to identify herself, but the 'Mrs. Sikand' rankled her. Why couldn't she be just – Maya? She had tried being 'just Maya' at a government office recently trying to get a ration card made to prove that she was a 'bonafide' resident of Delhi and had failed miserably.

"Aage peechhe kuch nahi? (No prefix or suffix?)", the government official on duty had asked her through betel stained teeth, sizing up Maya's hour glass figure, her designer sunglasses firmly pushing back her lustrous hair. A few appraisal stares and fruitless verbal exchanges later, Maya had no choice but to identify herself either as the wife of the man she had loved deeply or the daughter of the man she hated. The love and the hate both hurt.

Mrs. No-one

Maya took a deep breath and braced herself to answer the next batch of questions prescribed as part of the adoption procedure. She laid a leather folder containing neatly clipped papers on the dusty desk— her identity proof, bank statements, educational certificates and numerous medical reports that proved the verdict justifying the decision to adopt – Maya was incapable of having a biological child, post the botched abortion years ago. Another neatly labelled folder comprising papers had Maya's marriage certificate, the court order granting divorce to Rahul and Maya, references from other 'bonafide' and 'respected' Indian citizens vouching for Maya's character, work-life and general behavioural qualities conducive to child rearing.

"Reason for divorce?" the official queried again in a tone that seemed to suggest that Maya's husband must've been an idiot to let go of a 'hot number' like this one.

"Mutual consent as a result of incompatibility" said Maya pursing her lips parroting the reason block printed on the court order. Given Maya's deep rooted desire to avoid washing dirty linen in public and of course, Rahul's request to keep things simple, they had agreed to keep Malathy and the episode out of the divorce proceedings. As the court official had read out the judgement, narrating the fairy tale account of Rahul and Maya's marriage, the years of happy married life and the development of 'irreconcilable differences' that ultimately led to a separated existence and thus divorce was being granted to them, Maya had not been able to stop the tears- in full public view. She had no idea what Rahul was feeling. Was it the male prerogative of internalizing pain and regret, of being brave and strong and being the master of masking emotion or was it the spell of the overwhelming attraction he felt for Malathy? When Maya looked up through her film of tears, Rahul seemed to be intently studying the wooden carving on the ancient platform where the judge sat. His expression could only be described as deadpan.

That had been two years ago. At some point, she could not remember when, she had finally stopped bursting into tears at the, mention of Rahul, divorce or any, of her tearjerker memories. She no longer burst into tears but was overcome by a sense of defiance and intense irritation at nosy questions on her personal life. Life had given her an opportunity to do what she wanted to do, not what her mother thought was good for her or what Rahul thought was good for him and thus – them. Adopting a child was the most important of them all and Maya was determined to take on the system and have her way.

The official had finished with Maya's file. Maya thought he'd just sign and stamp whatever form he was supposed to and let her get on with it. Instead, he pushed the file aside and peered into Maya's face, his chin resting in the cup of his nubby palm.

"Madam, *mushkil hai*. (It is difficult). Very difficult. You are working in private college. Private means no end time for work, no casual leave, no privileged leave, LTA (Leave travel allowance) they give but you do not take. You take LTA and go and you come back and *phut*, someone else has come and taken your assignment. More job, more work, fast promotion. What to do? I know everything Madam, my sister's son working in private. Very good allowance, but this life is better no of ours? Teatime, little *gup shup* (chatting), file closed. At least we are home for festivals; at least we have time for our children. Madam, management of baby and private job very difficult Madam," he sighed.

"We are trying Madam, to give orphan children good good homes, where mother has time to do mother's job of baby minding. Working couples also not preferred. Working mother, plus alone Madam, very difficult for baby. How you will manage? Plus paperwork not complete Madam. By the time the paperwork is complete, baby becomes available, medical, everything, you might be nearing middle age Madam. When baby finishing school, going to college, you will be getting old. Difficult Madam. Of course you are not looking your age at all, but papers have everything you know..." he concluded with a dramatic sway of his bald head, handing the file back to Maya.

Maya was disgusted. Was there no end to the chauvinism, the repeated references to her single self, her age... and this was the fourth adoption

Mrs. No-one

agency she had approached. Polite refusals citing a 5-year-waiting period, the absence of 'suitable babies', the veiled reference to 'financial support for the upkeep of the adoption centre', numerous papers to be submitted, proofs to be procured...

If Maya had still been married to Rahul (irrespective of whether Rahul would have actually made time to care for the child), the adoption would have been so much easier. They would have fit the criteria for ideal adoptive parents – affluent, both healthy, mother not working so as to be able to dedicate herself to child rearing. Maya did not meet any of these criteria any more. But the critical bit was, if she was still with Rahul, she would not be visiting adoption agencies at all, for Rahul did not want a child. She had not had a choice but to leave Rahul. She had not had a choice but to take up a job when Rahul's promised support started waning. She simply did not have the energy or the spite in her to sue Rahul for the alimony due. More practically, if the case dragged on for years, she had no money to pay lawyer fees. And if she wanted to give the child a good life, she would have no choice but to keep the job. Fighting tears of frustration, Maya gathered her papers, muttered a crisp, "Thank you" and walked out.

24

DIWALI

It was the first day of the festival of lights – Diwali, a day pronounced auspicious by the Panditji (Hindu priest) Bua had been conferring with since an excited Maya rung her to convey that the adoption process had finally come through, the paperwork, medical examination, the numerous checks on Maya… everything was done.

It was a year since Maya had walked out of the last adoption agency office in disgust. Refusing to give up, Maya had finally approached Mrs. Mitra. Apart from being an astute businesswoman, Mrs. Mitra was known for her philanthropy. The Corporate Social Responsibility (CSR) ventures of her group of companies and the charitable trust she had set up in her late husband's memory, generously donated to several organizations every year. Preeti had been confident that her mother-in-law would be able to speak to some people and help with Maya's adoption process.

"I'm not shopping Mrs. Mitra. I'm not going about defining specifications and picking an attractive package. I am looking for a child who doesn't have parents to fulfil my dream of being Mum. Why can't these people understand that? And who are they to decide whether a single Mum would look after a child properly? Didn't you and others like you do a brilliant job of being a single parent? Or is it more honourable to be a widow than to be divorced and still want to be Mum?" Maya's poise had given way to anger at the system. She was seething,

"I have all the documents they wanted. I don't have the financial security that I had when I was married, but I am doing an honest day's job. I don't want to go about taking the wrong path and for you to seek favours from someone for something I want badly," said Maya, wishing she had not had to request favours for what she believed should have rightfully been hers.

Described as the Iron lady or even 'Dragon Queen' among people who worked with her and had experienced her wrath, Mrs. Mitra gave Maya a long hard stare.

"You've got spunk Maya and don't let anyone touch your confidence. You know and I know that there is a multitude of babies across the world and especially in this country who badly need a good home. For every child trafficking and adoption scandal that makes the headlines every few years, there are a 100 other organizations doing great work. They have their limitations, they need funds, and they need fool proof systems. I'm not a great fan of the country's legal infrastructure you know. But I do know that it is the Government's duty to protect the orphans of the country from exploitation by ruthless individuals posing as adoptive parents. Let the Government do its job. Our country's legal system does have the provision to enable a single woman or man to adopt. And I'm not about to break any law, for you or for anyone else. It is just the social biases we have to take care of. There is no law against social bias, bad vibes or scrutiny by oily clerks. Some day that will change. Till then, ignore it and get on with what you want most out of life. And leave your papers here," her monologue delivered in an even tone, Mrs. Mitra stood up.

Taken aback but suddenly hopeful, Maya knew the interview with the 'Dragon' was over. She murmured a word of thanks and stepped out of Mrs. Mitra's elegantly done up spacious office.

True to her promise, Mrs. Mitra had set the wheels of the adoption machinery rolling. In just three weeks, Maya was called to visit Bal Udyan, an orphanage in Mumbai. Maya spent two hours at Bal Udyan, registering her name as an adoptive mother, filling out the forms and of course interacting with the dynamic lady social worker Savitatai who had been running the orphanage for two decades.

A month later, with the initial paperwork in place and Savitatai's exhaustive grilling of Maya on why she really wanted to adopt concluded, Savitatai finally smiled and held out her hand,

"Maya ji. You come strongly recommended by Mitra Madam. Of course Mitra Madam has done so much for our organization over the years. But most important, I am now convinced that one of my babies, whenever she arrives here, will have a courageous and caring mother. And on a lighter note, elephants have a 22-month pregnancy. I will try to shorten it for you as much as possible!" After those encouraging words from Savitatai, the mother of many, Maya knew she had made it… well almost. Excited, Maya's preparations for the baby began in full swing.

It was time to watch the pennies again. Not having realized how frequent the trips to Mumbai would be, Maya would sometimes take the train to Mumbai or book flights at odd hours on low cost carriers. She also had to accumulate days off she was entitled to at college, take additional lectures for the students due to appear for the University exams (what if the baby appeared bang in the middle of the curriculum completion frenzy). Then there was the adoption paperwork all over again, consultations with lawyers, the availability of a girl child, more paperwork…

And now, finally, 11-months later, there was good news. Thrilled at the prospect of finally bringing home the child she had yearned for 15 years, Maya intended to take the next flight to Mumbai and bring the baby home as soon as they would let her. But Bua would have none of it.

"I'm old Maya, but not that old. With Jyoti and Suketu away in America and their little boys speaking only in English, not liking Indian food, not wearing Indian clothes, not really interested in festivals, I hardly ever get a chance to pamper my grandchildren. But this little grand-daughter of mine will have the best this Grandmother of hers can give her. I'll be in Delhi a few days before Diwali and I'll ask Panditji to give us auspicious dates to bring the young one home and a good alphabet for the name as well. You call her what you want but she must have a proper *naamkaran* (naming ceremony) and an auspicious name as well," Bua hung up, bubbling over with with all that planned to do.

And here she was, waiting at the doorstep when Maya and the baby arrived home, tired after the flight, directing Maya's new maid to perform a proper welcome.

"Now put a little *kumkum* (red powder) on the baby's forehead, just a little. Sprinkle a few grains of the coloured rice on her head, the oil lamps should be glowing now, move the *thali* (plate) clockwise. Now do the same for the baby's mother. It is such an auspicious occasion, use your right hand!" she clicked her tongue in despair at the maid's ignorance of Hindu customs and in the same breath, to Maya,

"If your Phuphaji was alive, I would have performed the welcome myself, worn auspicious bright pink. What do I do? The traditions ingrained in me do not allow a widow to perform auspicious ceremonies. But don't let any of these inhibitions we grew up with hold you back Maya. You have displayed courage. Don't let any traditions hold you back. One fine day, when this little one grows up and gets married, you must perform the *Kanyaadaan* yourself. (The rite of passing on the responsibility of a daughter to a husband and the in-laws, traditionally performed by a bride's father or a married couple, but not by widows)."

Touched by the ceremonious welcome, Maya giggled.

"Bua, the child is 5 months old! Why are we discussing her wedding?" Undeterred, Bua turned and walked away, commanding Maya to put her right foot into the house first!

For the next few weeks, Bua was the boss of the household, "training the maid" to sterilize the baby's milk bottles correctly, holding her up and massaging her tiny back till she burped and was to be put down in her baby cot. Unable to sit on the floor or cross her legs due to arthritis, she commanded the maid to drag a straight-backed chair into the bathroom so that she could supervise the baby's daily oil massage and bath rituals. Maya had her set of instructions too— which vegetables and lentils were good for the baby in mashed form, what was to be observed at festivals, how Maya herself should be eating the nutritious *laddoos Bua* had made.

"They are little bombs of molasses, dry fruits and semolina made in *ghee* (vegetable fat). You know I don't eat sugar and fat Bua. All that's for new Mums who've gone through the pain and discomfort of labour Bua, not for me!" Maya protested eyeing the rows of sweet balls in the steel box Bua had produced from her suitcase.

"The labour's just the beginning of discomfort Maya. Sleepless nights, illnesses, colic, emerging teeth, tantrums, the cycles of feeding and changing… you have to go through them all. That is why you are the mother. And new Mums need good care and energy restoration. Not for nothing do we have the tradition of girls being with their parents for the birth of the first child. And you are going to do the job of a mother and a father. Let go of your fancy diets for once and build your strength for the arduous path of parenthood," Bua's face softened as she squeezed her arm affectionately.

It was three weeks since the baby arrived home. Bua was in conference with her Pandit again. All the orphanage records could tell Maya what was the approximate month of her birth. But Bua declared that the date and time of her birth would have helped in drawing up her astrological chart but it did not matter. Panditji would find a way, he always did.

Besides, like was the case with all the children in the orphanage, Urja looked younger than she was. Though thin, she was a sprightly baby, with bright dark eyes and frizzy dark brown hair. When she was hungry, her lusty cry could be heard right across in the apartment next door. The cry grew louder as Maya

Diwali

or the maid appeared with the milk bottle. Her anxious eyes would follow the bearer of the bottle as she straightened the sheets, changed her nappy, and checked that the milk was of the right temperature. The cries grew louder and louder and only stopped after the nipple of the milk bottle was safely in the child's mouth. It was almost as if the child was afraid that the bottle of milk that was tantalizingly close would not go to her after all.

But unlike other children her age who often demand to be cuddled, kept warm or simply looked at and spoken to, this little baby seemed quite content to be left alone, curiously staring at the assortment of toys and colourful pictures that Maya had filled her room with. Despite the joy of having her very own little one finally, the cycle of changing/feeding/burping/doctor visits... was taking its toll on Maya's health. Things would settle down she knew and she would eventually get less jumpy every time the baby uttered a whimper. Besides, she was not a lithe 20-year-old anymore and her energy was definitely on the decline.

But even as she brushed the sleep out of her eyes and obediently consumed the glass of milk and the two soaked almonds Bua had laid out for her, Maya smiled,

"I'd never trade these moments of motherhood for anything!" she sighed.

Bua had finally finished her deliberations on the phone. She laboriously made her way to the drawing room and heaved herself onto the sofa announcing,

"The name can begin with U."

"Not too many modern names begin with that alphabet but there are some older ones. Ulka, Ujwala, Urmila... maybe Unnati. They all have lovely meanings— brightness, dawn, progress... Maybe you should pick one of these just for the naming ceremony and actually call her something else, some modern name?" Bua looked anxious as she knew Maya would want something unique and trendy. There wasn't much of a choice given this problematic difficult alphabet – U.

Maya smiled, patting Bua's hand. Her days of being embarrassed to be seen with Bua with her impossibly gaudy nylon saris, of not using the hideous outfits Bau used to gift her when she was little… were long over. The race for the 'cool quotient' did not matter anymore and she did want to make Bua happy after all the affection she had showered on her all her life.

"OK Bua, let's see what we can find." Maya picked up her laptop to surf through the baby names websites she had been browsing through for months now. With Bua peering over her shoulder, sceptical about what this contraption could actually produce in terms of decent Hindu names, Maya skimmed the website for girls name starting with 'U'. There were hardly 15 entries and there it was. Maya clutched Bua's hand in delight,

"Urja means energy Bua. Of course, right now the brat saps all the energy from her fast-aging Mum but she signifies energy for me. Energy, enthusiasm, hope for the future... the reason to not just exist but lead a life full of zest – Urja she will be!"

25

CANDLE AND THE MOTH

"What I saw in the mirror today... was the most sensitive and gentle human being I have ever known. Who yearns to feel what I feel, with the light of radiance on his face.

Was it the soft light in my hair or the tender look of adoration on his face... that made me look... Well, for the first time in so long... in my own eyes... Well, beautiful!"

This was Maya writing to Kay, a spontaneous four-liner describing a memorable moment of their time together. When Maya stood before her canvas the next morning, the four-liner would take the shape of an evocative silhouette of two figures before a mirror.

Painting— though Rahul had always encouraged her to do her own thing and had even been extremely proud of what she did, Maya's own obsession with not making the mistake her own mother did—of surpassing the man in her life, had always made her hold back. And as long as she did not make much money out of her creative pursuits, nor chase giddy heights of fame as an artiste, Maya had told herself there was no danger of that happening and that her marriage was safe.

With Kay, it was different. She wanted to prove she was good; in fact even better than what he thought her to be and said she was. Kay was as much a man as Rahul with the same pride and intolerance for "partners surpassing them" as so many men did. But with a 20-year head start, Kay not just indulged, but took wonderful care of her. As an accomplished celebrity musician, Kay was nowhere near feeling insecure because of Maya.

Their relationship, what Kay had termed a "celebration of her intellect and the worshipping of her inner as well as physical beauty," had Maya blossom into her creative best.

Maya and Kay had met years ago when Maya and Rahul were the guests of honour at one of Kay's music concerts. Over the years, they ran into each other often. Some of the concerts were followed by charity dinners for select guests and any such event in this genre was incomplete without Maya.

At these social events, Kay was usually surrounded by eager music lovers as well as those who liked to be seen as music lovers, hanging on to every word he uttered. Apart from his soul stirring music, Kay's dark, intense eyes and his shoulder-length thick dark hair greying at the temples, often let loose at performances, were attractive to so many in the audience. But Maya was wrapped up in Rahul and still swept up by the illusion of her high profile marriage. She would be polite, interested, cordial, friendly and gracious, smiling coyly at a compliment... but once again she would yearn for the Rahul she loved and sorely missed.

Like everyone else in the circuit heard, Kay heard of the Malathy scandal too. The whisper campaign had conveyed it all - Maya had moved out of the mansion. She had taken up a small apartment. She probably still had her diamonds, but the Rs. 15000/- per head charity shows were not her scene any more. But Maya, like so many other music lovers, never missed the opportunity to listen to Kay every time he performed in Delhi. So when Kay spotted Maya in the audience at a concert he was doing free of charge in memory of his own music Guru, it was not a big surprise. During the intermission, he had one of the student volunteers at the show deliver a short note to her.

"It is heartening to see that the demands of social graces are no match for the all encompassing worship of music. Could I have the pleasure of your company tonight at a small dinner with select art lovers after the event?

—Kay"

Maya was moved and flattered. Listening to Kay's music free of charge was a rare treat and the venue was buzzing with a disciplined, orderly but large crowd. The seating was Indian style – cotton mattresses spread out on the floor covered with milk-white bed sheets and each row was ear-marked with stuffed cotton bolsters. Like the other music lovers, Maya sat upright cross-legged, her embroidered cotton *duppatta* wrapped around her shoulders. Of course, none of the charity event regulars would venture out to something that clearly cost nothing and was not considered high profile to merit attendance. But Kay had still noticed her presence.

Even when she was married to Rahul, Maya's hectic social evenings comprised dinners, charity events, art gallery evenings, theatre openings, music concerts, art auctions… almost everything that was anything, had Maya there. But all of these engagements carefully skirted around Rahul's busy schedule. Maya would attend if Rahul wanted to go too. If Rahul seemed faintly hesitant about wanting to attend any of these, Maya would send in her apologies well in advance with a formal handwritten note and a token amount to support the event in any case. If Rahul was travelling she would still attend. But if Rahul was in Delhi and home, never ever would Maya be away even if he was cooped up in his study, working at his laptop. She would lie down on the couch in the study and read, embroider or occasionally sketch a personalized birthday card for one of their friends, periodically disappearing into the kitchen to get Rahul a mug of hot chocolate or a bowl of cashews.

This evening, like all other evenings in her life now, there was no Rahul to wait up for, no menus to plan, no holiday to book, but just her tastefully done up but small apartment to go home to. Maya smiled at the young volunteer and asked him to convey to Kay that she would see him outside the greenroom after the event.

Maya

It was a lovely evening, with Kay and just a few of his *Guru bandhus* (fellow students of Kay's late music teacher). She recognized none of the others. None of them had attained the giddy heights of fame that Kay had. Among them was a music teacher, a harmonium player who accompanied several vocalists, even a software engineer who pursued his passion for music in his spare time. Maya was surprised and pleased to see the camaraderie that still existed among them and thoroughly enjoyed the conversation flitting around the arts. Nobody spoke of buying farmhouses, trips abroad, or made small talk about clients, high flying careers and international schools for children. Nobody asked and Maya too momentarily forgot her former social identity – Mrs. Maya Sikand, wife of high flying IT industry honcho – Rahul Sikand.

Days after that fun-filled evening, the gifts began to arrive, a tiny box of Belgian chocolates fashioned in the shapes of different musical instruments, a delightful music disc comprising rustic Portugese music, and a beautifully carved jewellery box in the shape of a guitar. These were always artfully wrapped and accompanied by a message in Kay's trademark flourish.

The years passed and Maya waded through the new set of challenges in her life, largely by herself but with the soft glow of Kay's remote presence in her heart.

Late one night, when she had just fallen asleep after soothing Urja through another nightmare, she was shaken awake by the persistent ringing of the telephone. The caller ID flashed Kay's name and she panicked, rushing to answer.

"*Mayaji, aapke naam* (in your name)…" and Kay hummed a soulful bar of music. Maya knew Kay had been grappling with this particular composition for the background score of an art film and had been particularly irritable when she last spoke to him. He had finally found just the right slots to seat the magical seven notes in and was overjoyed with the result.

"It's lovely Kay, suits the mood of the film you described perfectly," Maya smiled, suppressing a yawn, not having the heart to point out time zone differences and that she had art college and mundane graphic design lessons to attend the next morning.

"It's great being a companion… no fun being a wife', Maya used to tell herself all through the years when she resented Malathy's presence in Rahul's life. But now, here she was a companion who brought great joy to Kay.

When she realized it, Maya was astounded at the ease with which men could get into relationships while still intending to stay in 'good marriages' in the long term.

Kay did too. Kay had family back in America and he insisted that his marriage was in the best possible shape it could be. He insisted he was a good husband and father, though often absent due to his performances across the globe.

From being a devoted wife, who didn't just pretend to, but actually believed that what she shared with Rahul was incomparable to any other man she had ever met, Maya found herself giving her all… all over again, to Kay.

26

HAPPY BIRTHDAY URJA!

It was Urja's fourth birthday and Maya had pulled out all stops in organizing a 'monsoon theme' party. The venue she had picked had a children's play area done up in blue and yellow with toad-stools and the backdrop of a rain-forest. The children were having a gala time clambering up and down a mini climbing-square, swishing down bright coloured snaky slides and thumping about on a huge cloud of a trampoline. Disney characters waded through the crowd, shaking hands with the delighted children, painted smiles and dimples on the huge painted masks camouflaging their sweaty, tired faces underneath.

Rahul's promises of ensuring that Maya got her due were on shaky grounds. But Maya was determined that Urja should have the best. And if there was no Dad to hang up paper buntings and balloons in a re-decorated drawing room, it was just as well. Maya would ensure that little Urja had a birthday party any four-year-old would dream of.

Preeti was down with a cold and called in to say that she didn't want to pass it on at the party – especially with so many children around. Preeti's teenagers, though well-behaved and fond of 'Maya Aunty', had made a quick

Happy Birthday Urja!

appearance, swept up a delighted Urja with shrieks of 'Happy birthday!' deposited the lovely gift Preeti had wrapped, grabbed a plate of snacks and dashed for the exit in 30 minutes flat! There was Mrs. Mitra of course, well turned out as usual, dressed in an elegant pale yellow and bright blue sari dutifully following the 'Happy monsoon colours' dress-code specified on Maya's customized party invitation card. The lady had parked herself on one of the larger toad-stools, in a visible corner of the play area. Children walked in with mothers, nannies and in case there were siblings in the same age-group, two nannies! That was the latest rage in Delhi circles. A household retinue was considered incomplete without a cleaner, cook, chauffer per car and a live-in nanny per child. And the live-in nannies accompanied them everywhere – school, nursery, shopping excursions, family holidays and of course – birthday parties. Each nanny carried a well-equipped handbag stuffed with the standard outing gear- diapers if the child still needed them, an extra set of clothes, socks, bibs, napkins, water-bottle and the child's favourite snacks. It was always best to have the snacks handy if little baba or baby refused to sample any of the goodies laid out at the party and threatened to throw a tantrum.

Perched on her toadstool, Mrs. Mitra smiled warmly at the mothers walking in, waved at the children and nodded at the nannies, making a mental note of keeping an eye on them and reporting any untoward behaviour to Maya. She needn't have worried. Most of the nannies attended at least one such party per month and were familiar with the drill:

1. Sit quietly in a corner.
2. Don't let your ward out of sight.
3. When it was time to eat, fill the child's plate.
4. Try to feed him if he refuses to eat.
5. Generally sit around and chat with the other maids till it was time to leave.

Maya

Happy and of course touched to see that Mrs. Mitra had taken on the grandmotherly role of overseeing the goings on in the children's section and with Urja happily bouncing on the cloud-shaped trampoline, Maya was about to step away to check on the puppet show arrangements when she was interrupted by a bellowing voice.

"Hello Maya, looking thin as usual huh! *Abhi to* now you are Mummy, you should look like us Mummies no?" it was Charu Batra, a swelling mass of bright pink silk, jingling bangles, dangling ear-rings, grinning broadly. Before Maya could respond, the pink mass turned to her entourage. A uniformed chauffer carrying a colossal gift-wrapped package, two nannies scrambling to restrain two plump adolescents dressed in identical silver sequined space-suits. So far so good… none of this was a surprise for Maya. Themes and dress codes held no significance for Charu. She usually flaunted her latest acquisition however inappropriate it may appear for the occasion! And her two pampered sons – the silver suits must have cost a bomb and if that is what they wanted to wear this evening, the two nannies had no choice but to have them ready for the little babas. Urja's birthday celebration was soon turning into a Delhi nanny congregation, but in case of Charu's kids, Maya was thankful for the presence of their two guardians. Maya recalled the story a few years ago - Charu's younger son Jugal had once bitten a child at a birthday party while Charu blissfully munched on her *paneer pakoras*!

The surprise package as such stood a head above Charu, dressed in blue jeans and a pale blue polo neck T-shirt.

"Meet Kishore, my brother-in-law from England. He was feeling very shy to come with us. I told him, this is India. Party means all are welcome, with family and friends. Maya is little modern. She did not print 'All are welcome' on the invitation card. But so what, Indian hospitality is Maya's plus point no?" breathless with these pronouncements, Charu gladly ambled across to sink into a chair and grab the welcome drink proffered by a waiter.

"It is nice of you to have me Ma'am. With Charu *bhabhi* it is so difficult to get in a word, even if it is a plain 'No'", smiled Kishore quickly explaining his presence in an Indo- British accent.

Happy Birthday Urja!

"Oh it is a pleasure to meet you. You're most welcome. Do help yourself and enjoy the party," said Maya smiling graciously, excusing herself to see to the puppeteers.

The puppet show concluded and the children clapped in glee. Maya wheeled in the customized birthday cake. It had a little statue of Urja herself holding a cream-frosted pink umbrella while she hopped across puddles of chocolate sauce. Four green frog-shaped candles sat grinning around the charming monsoon scene. The Mums, the nannies, Mrs. Mitra, the kids and yes, Kishore (now having realized that he was the only adult male in room) gathered around the cake for a feisty rendition of 'Happy birthday to you!' Urja blew out the candles, plunged the knife into the luscious cake and promptly opened her mouth looking at Maya expectantly. "Clearly a pro at the birthday party scene", thought Maya as she fed her a piece of cake smiling indulgently. The other little party pros had their mouths open, waiting to be fed the first piece of cake. Mrs. Mitra bustled about offering to cut the cake into little pieces and feed the party pros when Urja announced,

"Momsy first!" She picked up a piece and held it up to Maya's lips.

It was such a tiny gesture, but touched Maya deep within and she suddenly found her eyes well up with tears. Maya picked up a tissue and stepped away.

27

ABYSS

"It's great being a companion, no fun being a wife", Maya had thought during her best moments with Kay.

"And why not?" Like any other married couple, Rahul and Maya's marriage had its share of spontaneous moments, shared responsibilities, disappointments, sacrifices and expectations. In retrospect, Maya wondered if she alone had ended up making all the sacrifices in her desire to surpass all of Rahul's expectations. Had Maya been carried away by her fervent desire to be the best at everything... best socialite, best hostess, best wife? Had she offered so much of herself on a platter, much more than was actually needed? Did true love have limits to how much was needed to be given and received?

But Maya had failed somewhere. If she hadn't, would Rahul not be with her at this very moment?

Her thoughts drifted to Kay and Maya wondered if the idea of a perfect marriage really was a myth. Maya had walked through life spotting couples who appeared happy and capturing what they appeared to be doing right in a relationship. Just when she thought she had got things right, life had begun to spin horribly out of control.

Was she doing the same thing with Kay – wrapping herself around his life when he had clearly defined the boundaries of his life she could not permeate? Maya would accompany Kay to musical evenings, high profile events, attend his important performances but he would not make an appearance at the most important event in her life – Urja's party.

Diwali, New Year's Eve, Christmas holidays were all 'family time' for Kay and Maya was certainly not family.

Had she not known this? Had she learnt nothing in her life about being vulnerable and had she opened herself up to hurt again? For the first time in years, Maya began to question the supposed strength and stability of her own mind. She had borne it all alone – the pain, sorrow and then the guilt that the horrific experience of the abortion had brought, the shock of her mother's death and the loss of her entire family in one shot. The Rahul she once knew had been with her then but had she really allowed herself to collapse, let others see these raw wounds and let Rahul be the gallant one and take care of her broken mind?

Kay had captured the beauty of Maya's mind and unleashed the talent that Maya had hidden from Rahul and in a way, herself too. But Kay's affection had its boundaries – the framework demanded Maya fit in. If she didn't, he would not change. Whenever Maya asked Kay about his wife, he would say that a 'good marriage may mean different things to different people' and that the relationship he shared with his wife was on a 'different plane'. Still, Maya questioned her own role as the 'other woman'. Was she causing an upheaval in an otherwise happy marriage? Was she putting Kay's family through the trauma she had experienced herself? The truth was that if it had not been for Maya, it would have been someone else who occupied that 'special' place in Kay's life. The special place that was on a 'plane' different from the one he shared with his wife. That place was of the muse.

Rahul was so consumed by his attraction for Malathy that he did not care what Maya thought or did. By walking out, Maya had just made things simple. But Kay's wife would never make anything simple, nor would his children and his larger than life persona that dominated the world of Indian music. More important, though Kay never spelt it out, that is just the way Kay probably wanted it, just like Rahul had, a specialist to look after each of the aspects of his life.

For all the compliments Kay showered on Maya, in his life of performances, awards, fame, family and home, Maya realized that she barely had a transitional miniscule role. Maya finally acknowledged the painful truth… it was time to exit. And once again, it was Maya who had to muster the courage to get up and walk away.

The years of the poised socialite appearance had brought the pretence of being composed, dealing with sorrow, pain, joy and exhilaration with dignity.

Now there was no Rahul, no Kay and the realization that Maya actually was not the composed, dignified prima donna she had pretended to be. The tears flowed and Maya slipped, slowly into an abyss, deep down below.

28

BE PRACTICAL

It was the day after Urja's birthday and Charu Batra was on the phone.

"*Bachha log* (The children) enjoyed a lot Maya. Your guest entertainment skill is still intact huh Maya. Did Urja like our gift? Jugal's Papa got it all the way from Bangkok you know. Very expensive these things, but I told Jugal's Papa that our Urja baby must have the best. So much Maya is doing for the poor child. This is our little contribution no? Jugal's Papa is very busy you know. I told him what a wonderful party he missed," gushed Charu.

Maya had long stopped getting upset at such pronouncements from Charu. That was just the way Charu was made. Charu's ostentatious behaviour and the absence of tact could result in soaring levels of irritation, but she did not necessarily mean ill. In fact, the Charu experience once in a while gave Maya a sense of reassurance in the consistency that she had sought so desperately and had not found. Charu was loud and she always would be. Charu was not expected to display the chameleon behaviour that Maya had seen in her marriage and the subtle but sure cooling of relationships with several of her well-heeled contacts when Maya ceased to be the CEO's wife.

Maya

The job at the art scollege, graphic design certifications, Urja and of course the alarming situation with money, meant that Maya had given up many of the indulgences of being Mrs. Sikand. Kitty parties were out. Certain that the ladies would commence animated discussion on the state of Maya's marriage as soon as she was out of earshot, Maya did not miss them. Maya's grand dinners and patronizing new musicians and artists was definitely out. Of course close friends were most welcome in Maya and Urja's new cosy home, but the resources, time and enthusiasm for grand do's simply had dried up. And most shockingly, takeaway dinners for friends dropping in, did not seem such a 'down market and inhospitable' concept to Maya anymore!

Charu had taken to dropping in (thankfully, without her two terrors and their respective nannies), often with some homemade sweetmeat or the other for Urja, a shiny little ghagra choli (traditional Indian outfit) for the child during Diwali and a crate of mangoes in summer. When she had first got wind of Maya's plans to adopt a little girl, Charu had vehemently tried to dissuade her.

"What is the need for social work? Think about yourself. You are quite young Maya, so fair, tall, slim, well educated, that too with no issues. *Aajkal* (nowadays) there is no age limit. If you had family, they would have had no trouble at all finding an eligible match for you. *Tera kuch karnaa chaahiye* (Something must be done with you)!" she declared, helping herself to another slice of fruit Maya had placed before her. Maya cringed. Charu made her sound like a standard Indian matrimonial advertisement (ones that described dark skinned girls as 'wheatish complexioned' and 'Convent educated' to denote that they could speak in English). And Charu's last statement made her sound like some kind of valuable commodity that needed to be dispensed with!

Ignoring the insinuations and overtones, Maya had dismissed Charu, firmly telling her that adopting a baby had nothing to do with social work, she had no interest whatsoever in getting married again and having a child was what she had yearned for years and she would!

Be Practical

Though it all sounded quite appalling, Maya could sense desperation in Charu's voice. Was Charu trying to say that her own husband had his own share of flings and even a mistress in Bangkok? Was she trying to convey to Maya that in walking out of her marriage, Maya had done what Charu wanted to, but could not do?

Maybe, years ago, Maya had sensed a similar sense of regret in another appalling statement Charu had made when she found out that Maya had walked out of her marriage.

"I think you could do it because you have good looks and education. A woman cannot just walk out of a marriage", Charu had declared at the 'condolence' kind of gathering of women who had come to see Maya at Preeti's home on hearing the shocking news of Maya's departure from the Sikand's mansion. Possibly sorely disappointed that Maya did not rave, rant, weep, shout, swear revenge at Rahul or slander Malathy's character, most of the women sipped the coffee Preeti offered and left shortly. Charu and a few others had stayed and spelt out many of the questions the others did not have the courage to, or were too dignified to mouth.

"What is the lady's name? Is she married? What does her husband do? Is she prettier than Maya? How did Maya find out what Rahul was up to? When did she first suspect something was on?"

Charu would have continued the interrogation even longer if Mrs. Mitra had not barged into the room giving Preeti a cold stare for being a weakling and letting the natters into her home in the first place!

"None of these things matter. What happened is between Rahul and me. If we both don't feel the love and need for companionship that we shared, there is no sense staying on in a marriage. It is the most painful thing I have ever experienced, but it is the only thing to do," Maya stood up, thanked them for coming to see her and walked away, leaving Preeti to play the good hostess and see Charu out.

That was years ago when Charu's blunt statements and relentless questions hurt. Over the years, Maya had got the sense of exactly where Charu's preposterous statements came from. Now Charu was on the phone again, match-making not in generic but specific terms.

"Living in England, Kishore is so broad-minded. He is willing to accept Urja though he has no issues of his own. He is owning many assets in England you know. He keeps telling me –

"Charu bhabhi you must come and be with me. Big house, big garden, restaurant, laundry, six shops and me alone!" gushed Charu enlisting her 'eligible' brother-in-law's assets.

1. Cars – Mercedes / BMW
2. Garden- sprawling
3. UK citizenship – granted
4. The paper-work for his disastrous marriage with the characterless woman- the divorce decree expected any moment, thankfully, short marriage and no issues from that worthless, gold-digging creature, still the woman was staking claim to three out of Kishore's six shops in Birmingham!" Satisfied with her eligibility checklist, Charu continued,

"I know he is not like Rahul. No fancy title and big company and everything posh. But he is doing very well, he is very rich, comes from a good family and you have the little girl to think of now. You have to settle now. Who will accept you? If you don't think practically now, all the good boys will be over," with a special emphasis on 'good boys' (classifying all prospective grooms as boys irrespective of their age), Charu paused in anticipation.

If Maya had not been so deep down in the abyss, this particular Charu experience would have been a great source of amusement, to be relished over a quiet coffee with Preeti, chewed over and brought up in endless conversations in future. But Maya was neither interested nor irritated or amused. Overcome by listlessness, Maya said nothing to Charu, hung up and refused to take any more calls.

29

WATER

Maya sat cross-legged on the sand, the expanse of the blue-green sea stretching out before her. She realized it had been a good decision to finally give in to Viv's persistent invitation to spend the holidays with his family in Goa.

Still deep within her abyss, Maya's mind had not let anything permeate the deathly stillness she had settled into. Urja would come running along and Maya would mechanically do whatever it was that she was needed to do and slip back into the depth of that stillness again. Preeti, Mrs. Mitra, even Charu Batra with her insistent phone call about how Maya and Kishore would make a perfect couple, had not shaken Maya's inert self.

The architecture career she had kicked away, the unborn baby who she felt she had not needed at that time, Rahul's love for her, Kay's transient need for her companionship, Mum who brought disaster on, Dad who left much before it was actually time for him to leave, Bua, whom she had wasted so many years shunning, were all dead.

With the wonderful warm welcome Bua had offered Urja four Diwalis ago, Maya had thought she had finally found a semblance of family. After the auspicious *naamkaran* (naming ceremony) Bua had wanted for Urja, Maya had tried to persuade Bua to stay longer in Delhi. But she would have none of it.

"You know I never liked Delhi, Maya. It was only because I was so fond of your father and you that I used to visit. I am happy with my courtyard and jhula (swing) in Pathankot. But you bring Urja to Pathankot during the summer break. It will do you both some good to get some fresh air away from this oppressive city," said Bua.

"Summer's too hot Bua and you know the situation with the power cuts. We'll plan to visit you next Diwali. Pathankot will be pleasant then. By then, Urja will be demanding fire-crackers, jumping on your rangoli designs and pouncing on your Diwali delicacies! And I love Indian clothes, so we can get a ghagra choli made for Urja. She'll be running about then. Meanwhile, Bua you take care of your knees and don't ignore the stomach ailment you seem to have been brushing away," said Maya visualizing how Urja's visit would brighten up an otherwise lonely Diwali for Bua. Smiling happily, Bua departed with a final hug for Urja and a final set of instructions for the maid about Urja's care.

Unfortunately, Bua had not survived another Diwali. And Maya did visit Bua in summer, but for the last time. The stomach ailment Bua had dismissed as one of those things, turned out to be a malignant tumour, far too advanced and ingrained into her organs to be surgically removed. A few months after Maya saw her off at Delhi railway station, Bua was found by her maid one morning doubling up in pain. She was rushed to the local hospital. The battery of tests ordered by the doctor revealed what anyone who had seen Bua just four months ago would have found impossible to believe. Bua had just a few painful months to live.

Jyoti and the kids could not make it as they had exams but Suketu flew down from the US for a fortnight and Maya too made a quick trip to Pathankot leaving Urja and the maid with Preeti for a day to see Bua in the hospital. The doctors had pronounced that nothing could be done for Bua except administering tranquillizers to help her bear the pain. Suketu's two weeks passed quickly. His IT company had a 'customer emergency' and he was called back. Maya too had returned to Delhi afraid to bring Urja to Pathankot in the severe heat and afraid to leave her behind with Preeti lest she cried for Maya and brought the house down.

Not having had the will to survive the next few months the doctors had predicted for her, Bua passed away the week after, surrounded by friends and neighbours, the multitude of relationships she had nurtured for years with affection.

Every Diwali and every summer thereafter, Maya thought of Bua's wrinkled face and felt her leathery, work-worn palm in hers, her otherwise large frame now shrunk, sunken in the metallic four-poster iron bed. When she heard of Bua's death a week later, she had wept, for all the years she had wasted in keeping Bua away. She made another quick trip to Pathankot for Bua's last rites performed by Suketu, who flew back to India from the US barely 48 hours after he'd just got in. Maya had sat still among the rows of mourners dressed in white, her head covered like the other women in the room softly repeating the Sanskrit verses recited by the Hindu priest. She returned to Delhi to see Urja down with a severe skin rash again. Doctor visits, maid problems, commitments at college, Urja cranky due to her illness again. Life swung back into the mundane and Bua was soon a tiny spec in the multitude of regrets that had stacked up in Maya's subconscious.

Today years later, as she sat cross-legged on the beach, the reasons for regret seemed to wash up ashore one by one like dead sea-life that the sea did not want to hold any more. There were so many regrets to leave behind...

Even the sophisticated image of Maya that she now saw had been a myth like the numerous 'friends' who cooled off when Maya ceased to be an important 'contact'.

She walked towards the waves, arms outstretched gazing out towards the horizon. Her tired eyes soaked in the vast, endlessness of the blue sky merging into the grey-blue sea somewhere beyond.

Maya

Her palms against the salty wind, she closed her eyes and sensed the momentum gathered by each approaching wave and its leisurely meandering as it subsided.

"This is life... something begins, gathers momentum, reaches a crescendo, crashes and meanders away. The meandering must be graceful too. This is so beautiful.

For all the sorrow and complexities in the world, the embrace of the water will bring peace. Let the sea swallow me. I will not mind," she thought as she walked on towards the sea. The waves gushed forth with immense force to embrace her.

30

LIFE

"Maya! Maya wait!"

The voice seemed to emerge from a deep dark cave. Or was she in the cave? And who was calling her? The voice had a musical, lyrical quality... was it Kay calling her from the cave? But Kay had gone away on a world tour with his family. And then he had a series of performances and album releases and workshops... he would not be back for 6 months.

Or was it Rahul? He had an ear for music and had even had some formal training in playing the tablaa as a child. But Rahul did not sound musical anymore, he sounded business like.

Or was it Dad? Maybe he had finally begun to speak again. May be they let him out seeing how harmless he was.

"Your Dad can't kill a cockroach without wincing!" her Mum used to say when Maya was little as Sunayana quashed the creatures with a determined swish of her broom in their dreary flat in Delhi. But Dad had killed Mum and now was he calling her? Or was Mum calling her, or was it Bua?

Maya

Maya walked on towards the horizon as if in a stupor. The water had nearly risen to her shoulders. She squeezed her eyes shut, the tears mingling with the salty froth from the sea waves and walked on.

"Mummy! Look, Mummy!" There was a delighted squeal and within seconds a cry of pain giving way to a high-pitched whimper,

"Mummy, Mummy, it's hurting!"

Startled, Maya turned. Through her film of tears, she spotted a tiny bright yellow and blue bikini clad form, holding out her arms towards Maya. Dragging her drenched floral skirt, Maya walked across towards the sand. Maya instinctively clutched at Urja's dimpled hands, brushing away the coarse sand that had pierced her palms and forearms when she stumbled. Urja hugged her tight and then held out her palm to Maya's lips.

Maya kissed the tiny palm and as she had always promised Urja, the magic kiss blew away the pain. More frightened than hurt and secure in her mother's arms, Urja flashed her a bright smile.

"Look what Kyla aunty bought us. A real sea shell necklace!" As Urja pranced about in her pretty blue and yellow beach sandals, her itsy bitsy sarong swaying in the wind, Maya's mind journeyed back from the deep sea, into the reality of price-tags, shopping and indulgence on attire.

In the past few years, she had made sure Urja owned all that she would wistfully gaze at as she browsed through the malls during her years of childlessness. It had been years since she evaluated price tags. When it came to Urja, she still refused to compromise. But when it came to shopping for herself now, once again she was the Maya who worked in the lawyer's office. In fact, this was the other extreme, way beyond frugality. It was listlessness. Maya would walk towards a mall and then simply walk past, suddenly feeling drained of the energy or the enthusiasm to traipse through the aisles of swish clothing, try on ill-fitting, over-priced ware and even worse, look at herself in the full length mirrors in the fitting rooms.

But when it came to shopping for Urja, Maya could never have enough!

"You know Maya, Urja couldn't care less whether the shoes she wears are branded or not. She doesn't need any more toys, clothes or shoes. She needs to feel confidence, joy and peace in the eyes of the one person she completely depends on – you," said Viv quietly walking up. Maya suddenly realized that Viv had been right behind Urja all this while. As he spoke, she understood that it had been Viv who had been calling out to her as she had walked towards the waves, not all the voices from the past she had imagined.

Having showed off her sea-shell necklace to her mother, Urja skipped away to join Kyla and the boisterous children as they built sand castles. Feeling drained, Maya sank onto the sand. Viv sat down beside her, carefully placing his most precious possession – his guitar case, next to him. Viv and Kyla had taken the kids along with Urja for one of their 'Yo' sessions with the village kids. The neighbouring village had been blessed with a diligent schoolmaster with a genuine interest in the overall progress of his lot. The gentleman had been grappling with the challenges of school infrastructure, the ignorance of the fisher folk and resistance from truant children themselves. But when Viv offered to teach English songs to his wards, he was delighted.

Urja was turning out to be quite a chatterbox and Viv described how she had demonstrated her prowess at 'teaching' her songs to the village kids. So 'Old Mac Donald' continued with a lesson from Viv set to the same tune:

"If you don't wash your hands before you eat… Eeaaeeaa oh!

Your hands have germs only soap can beat… Eaaeeaa oh!

And a germ of your finger, a germ in your mouth, a germ in your tummy, here a germ, there a germ… Eeaaeeaa oh!

Running to the loo

No food for you…

Clean hands, and then food from Mummy!"

Maya

"They play truant when they have the schoolmaster thrusting English grammar down their throats, but gyrate to my English numbers and even manage to take on Kyla's accent!" grinned Viv.

Maya gave him a wan smile. And then she asked him what they had never ever discussed all these years,

"Don't you have any regrets Viv? Even after all these years, I have seen very few couples share the chemistry, the understanding that you and Sneha seemed to have. Don't you miss her? Do you think life turned out well for her? Does she really love her husband? Can anyone love someone because someone else believes you should?"

"You remember Maya, there was something Sneha and I shared, something so beautiful that neither of us would have ever wanted to let go of. But young as we were, we knew it was a "here and now" relationship. We understood that so well that neither of us ever said it to each other," said Viv quietly.

"Sneha loved me. But the thought of letting go of the family and the trappings of all that life in that family offered, was unimaginable to her. And she never pretended otherwise. I missed Sneha, still do sometimes. But I have never tried to reach out to her. Does she love her husband? Maybe she grew to love him, I don't know. I lead a simple life Maya and whatever Sneha's life had in store for her, I do not want to introduce any complexity to it.

It is not just about the money and the social class that Sneha had taken for granted all her life. It is about what life meant to Sneha and what life meant to me. The way Sneha had grown up with diamonds, I grew up with music. For me, life without music is unimaginable. I could never have chucked my guitar to work in investment banking or do whatever else that gives one pots of money. Yes, Kay is in the socialite league today. But that's one Kay for the millions of aspirant musicians across the world who never ever make it big.

Like all talented and successful people, Kay has his aura, a spell that has his audience mesmerized. When Kay is in that zone, no one can penetrate the aura, not his family, not you, not anyone. Maya, you are an attractive woman, now of course regal looking!" he smiled, touching her arm warmly.

"I also know how sensitive you are and you have been hurt. The ravages of time add lines to our faces, set our lips and the corners of our eyes in certain ways. Yours have too. But you are still attractive and sensitive like the awkward teenager I met at Siya's birthday party years ago. You achieved all that you wanted to all those years ago. You smashed the glass ceiling Maya, right through the formidable barrier between the stable middle and the spurious upper class. You smashed the barrier and have now realized that there is nothing but emptiness to greet you here. It is nobody's home.

Rahul did not value your contribution to his success, his life, Kay did not let you touch his core, but do not undermine what you shared. They took away so much from you Maya. Will you not let their keepsakes flourish? With Rahul, you tried to hide every talent you had and still failed. You possibly surpassed him in everything you did. You might have lived in the illusion that you were playing the supportive coy wife, but everyone could see the star in you. And most of all, Rahul could!

The mind, especially your mind has strength that far surpasses any external force Maya. Don't undermine what you have. And don't ever think of giving up the beautiful life you have been blessed with. Not ever again," as Viv uttered the last sentence of his thought-provoking sermon, he gave a slight toss of his head to indicate the sea, patted Maya's damp hair, planted a soft kiss on her forehead, picked up his sandals and walked away across the sand to join the children.

Alone with the meandering waves again, Maya sighed.

How right Viv was and how right he always had been. Even at that disastrous birthday party years ago, Viv had been realistic, self-assured and happy while Maya had been awkward and eternally aspirant. All her life, she had been running to bridge the divide between what there was and what there could be. She needed to hold her ground, not run towards the waves that always seem to recede, be where she was and revel in what there is!

And most of all, Urja needed her. She looked upon her for every want. And what had Maya been about to leave behind to haunt her? The memory of the

Maya

only parent she had known walking away into the sea, seemingly possessed even as she sat sobbing by the seaside?

Urja's dark eyes concealed so much of the trauma she had witnessed as an infant. She did not deserve yet another traumatic experience that could scar her sanity for life. Urja did not deserve to be abandoned, yet another time.

Maya looked across the horizon again, beyond her beloved sea and whispered,

"The sea does not swallow. The sea brings peace."

31

THE POWER OF M

"Create a thousand memories that you will cherish forever," Kay had written to Maya one day. Then on, it was as if Maya discovered what "enjoying the moment" really meant. The first was to live every moment of the "here and now" relationship she shared with Kay without wasting precious moments on what would happen when Kay's family commitments and his travels for his next work would take him away. From unsuccessfully brushing away the cobwebs that the past left behind, Maya actually began to look forward to creating memories she could cherish and given the gift of her deft fingers, capture on canvas.

With his expansive world-view and a razor-sharp mind that mopped up experiences and doled out ideas with every passing day, such potent messages for Maya, came easily to Kay. And Maya deftly wedged these into her most telling works of art.

Kay's "thousand memories" message to Maya distilled into one of her most subtle but heart-wrenching works—'Candlelight'. The rich oil painting showed an extremely good-looking man and woman having a candlelight dinner in what seemed like the perfect setting. Amber and ochre drapes in the background,

Maya

a fine lace tablecloth, silver service and to complete the picture-perfect setting, a dark blue jewellery box placed at the centre of the table. Even through the grandeur of the setting and the couple's immaculate attire, Maya's paintbrush had managed to convey the fissure in the relationship. So subtle was it, that the impervious buyer may well miss it. But the art lover could not—the lady's lustrous eyelashes could barely shield the sidelong glance towards the diamond-studded watch encircling her wrist and the gentleman's thin pursed lips, had actually successfully suppressed a yawn!

At another time, Kay wrote,

"Learn to be truly nasty with people who deserve it." As she soaked in this one and it emerged in the form of a steel wire sculpture, Maya slowly began to unshackle herself from the 'loyalty' syndrome that still bound her to Rahul and the pretentious life she had left behind. Rarely with Preeti and almost never with Rahul had she unabashedly expressed the anger and the hurt that Rahul's behaviour had caused. Even now, what she primarily expressed was sorrow, and always spoke about how she would like to deal with the 'situation'. It was almost as if the 'situation', was a third-party entity, created with little or no influence by the real perpetuators - Rahul and Malathy. She would say she felt no bitterness towards Malathy or Rahul and in fact, hoped they would have a good life. But then, why did a vision of Rahul and Malathy married, creep into her dreams one night?

Kay's message about being "truly nasty" translated into an interesting steel-wire sculpture of a woman seated in the lotus position, embracing the globe. Instead of continents, there were frescoes of people, children, even animals and flowers. And firmly pressed under the woman's crossed knees were two snakes, their jaws wide open. The most interesting part of the sculpture though, was the woman's face: shoulder-length flowing hair, a soft, loving but strong smile and a bright red bindi painted on her forehead in the shape of the weighing scales- the symbol of justice.

Early in their relationship, Maya would endlessly talk to Kay of the immense joy little Urja brought into her life. After a rowdy children's party on New Year's eve, Maya was telling Kay about how it was nice being with "friends

The Power of M

who have stood by her and among people Urja really is happy with". Instead of a "Glad you had a good time" response, Maya was startled to receive a thought-provoking answer from Kay—

"Why does all the happiness in your life have to be a negation of your relationship with Rahul and a positive inference of Urja?" Soon enough, this took shape of a delightful water-colour showing a mermaid gleefully lost in the tossing of the blue waves around her with not a soul in sight. 'Hedonistic pleasure' she called it.

"Discover the power of M. Don't wait for a bee. Just flower on…," Kay had once written to her.

But somehow, Maya was unsatisfied with her creations inspired by the "flower on" message. The flowers and the bees she painted, appeared too sedate, too lifeless, too blasé for the immense power of that message and its relevance in Maya's life. Nothing, no mural, sculpture, multi-media painting or oil, seemed to work for Maya—until for the first time, she started doodling on a computer using animation packages. Unlike most others in her Delhi "wives" circuit, Maya had ensured that she was not just aware of the goings-on in the IT industry but was techno-savvy as well. The purpose at that time was to be able to show off to Rahul's colleagues and hold intelligent conversation about the latest tech gadgets during social gatherings.

And now, the computer had become a medium of expression. The flowers she created on the computer screen seemed almost obscene in their brightness, irreverent to the creator blessed with "controlled and subtle" aesthetic sensibilities, so insanely radiant that no one, not even their creator could stem the proliferation of these exotic blossoms. And the bees that had appeared so staid in the static image on canvas, came to life, displaying the inherent nature of bees, of flitting in and out lives, spurring procreation, but never staying still in a garden, never resting enough by a flower, to witness the beauty they helped procreate. The bee on Maya's computer screen flitted in and out, resting on a flower sometimes, or simply buzzing away. And the bee or otherwise, the blossoms continued to flower on…

32

AFTERLIFE

Maya was at a residential art workshop held in a picturesque guest house on the outskirts of Chandigarh. As primary sponsors, the Mitras had positioned it as a charitable event for Mumbai's street children to be exposed to art. Artists from across the country had assembled— the famous page 3 types, Indian artists based abroad, lesser known artists who welcomed the opportunity to hobnob with the glitterati, the sponsors from various business houses, socialite art collectors and of course art critics and features editors from prominent publications. And there were the street children from Mumbai, scrawny 8 to 13 year-old boys shepherded by the founder of the support shelter they all went to, a gentleman they all called Bhaiyya (older brother).

In her erstwhile socialite form, this event would have been a 'must-do' in Maya's social calendar. Today, Maya took in the snobbery of the mineral water bottles distributed, tinkle of finely crafted cups and saucers, dainty cucumber sandwiches and the glossy brochure on the 'field visit' to show the work done by the street children. The coffee break had injected the 'networking' virus and the furious proliferation of the social climbing epidemic was to continue through the weekend. Maya knew the tricks all too well. Spotting amicable journalists, prospective patrons, board members at award committees and decision makers in corporate houses, eager artists would swoop down to make a kill. Maya had been one such 'useful contact' and there was never a dearth of eager musicians and painters wanting to speak to her about promoting their work at her next do. But Maya had neither the means nor the intention to be a patron of the arts any more.

"Let me stick to appreciating works of art. I'm not up to the networking drill," Maya had said, declining Preeti's invitation to the workshop. As usual, Preeti's mother-in-law had swooped in,

"Corporate social responsibility (CSR) is not just about showing that you are doing something, it is about doing something as well. When we said we'd promote the cause of artists, we were not just talking about wine and cheese receptions, but getting tribal artists their due, bringing out the creative genius in the child on the street. Join in Maya. If you like what you see, or want to do things differently, come over to the office and we'll talk. Our CSR team needs a fresh set of people... there is so much to be done!" said the grand old Mrs. Mitra with a sweeping gesture. Maya could not decline the passionate appeal and here she was, along with the glitterati trouping into the 'conference arena' for deliberations on the 'Impact of ancient Indian sculpture on emerging art forms'.

The sessions were thought provoking and there was so much to observe and imbibe. What Maya enjoyed even more was mingling among the street children as they transformed the lawns of the guest house into a splash of colour. Vivid scenes from Bollywood movies, Indian festivals, the pantheon of Hindu Gods and Goddesses, a backdrop of Mumbai's famous Islamic shrine Haji Ali, coconut sellers on a beach... Like the others, Maya was aghast at the talent and creative genius that seemed to have been hidden by the grime of Mumbai's streets. Maya was struck by the sincerity in this creative expression – no thought for what is 'currently in' and 'what will sell', what colours are politically right, culturally acceptable, what was more likely to adorn the walls of an upmarket home, no making of statements, no pretence that your art or you were actually someone else. Maya weaved in and out of the maze of colour, stopping by to reflect on each creation and interact with its creator.

Maya

Mohammed, 11, originally from the state of Bihar, ran away from home when he was 9, to escape the beatings of his drunken father. Now makes a living by selling mineral water bottles and trinkets on Mumbai's sub-urban trains. He met one of Bhaiyya's colleagues from the shelter when he was making sand sculptures on Chowpatty beach. He has been a regular at the shelter since. This is his third art workshop.

Deepak, 8, was born in Mumbai's red-light area. He refuses to say any more about himself except that his mother is no more and she had told him his father had gone far away but definitely would come back some day. He has a part-time job washing up plates at a roadside food stall on weekends. He enjoys swinging on the handle bars of a moving train and feeling the sea breeze on his hair on a warm evening. He comes to the shelter every evening. He doesn't like the Maths and English lessons Bhaiyya insists they must take, but loves singing and playing with colour. But Bhaiyya insists on at least half an hour of those boring lessons before the paints are brought out. As she gathered nuggets of these stories of incredible grit, Maya felt a lump in her throat.

"If Mrs. Mitra had not done what she had slicing through the adoption agency red-tape, would her little Urja have grown up like this?" She was wondering why there were no little girls in the group from Mumbai when 'Bhaiyya' walked up to Deepak.

"Deepak, you must sign your name at the bottom of the painting. It's just six letters and you do know the alphabet now!" he said tousling the child's hair. Deepak grinned and started painting his name in English, sticking his tongue out in concentration.

"Bhaiyya this is Maya didi. She has never been on a local train in Mumbai!" said Deepak sounding incredulous at the situation.

"Hello Ma'am. Neil Pathak" he smiled. Maya smiled back politely enquiring about the work done by his organization, how many children came to the shelter in Mumbai, the role of art in their lives and finally, why were the girls excluded from this workshop. Neil answered patiently a little surprised that

Maya was spending time with the children, and had chosen to break away from the group and the frenetic photo opportunity chase that seemed to be underway on the other side of the lawns.

"Our non-profit organization– *Kalaa* (art), is five years old now. We've got a room under the foot-over bridge just outside a railway station in Mumbai. Our facility is very basic, but clean and safe. Trained social workers work in three shifts and I usually manage to reach the shelter after work in time for the Arts lesson. Children can drop in any time but usually they are busy at work or looking for work during the day. The room is most busy during the monsoon where a lot of brilliant works of art get created! But children do usually drop in on most evenings. If they do, they must first wash their hands and then can pick up any two pieces of fruit kept in the bowl in the corner. Not more than two as an enterprising street child would often pick up heaps and we found he had business plans of a roadside fruit stall brewing in his busy brain! They don't get chocolate or sweets at Kalaa, only fruit. Fruit is expensive in Mumbai, they could do with the nutrition and are also the least likely food item they would buy themselves," Neil smiled.

"A retired school teacher from a nearby convent comes in to teach English twice a week, two college students take up basic maths (the boys actually have rather good commercial sense but no long term vision) and science, mainly focussing on health and hygiene. The children have no time for school and though they are often fluent in 3 languages (English, Hindi and their mother-tongue), they are most reluctant to pick up a pen and paper. After this compulsory studies bit, the paints and modelling clay are brought out and that's what the children are really there for – free art paraphernalia. Kalaa mostly runs on personal or corporate donations.

There are no girls at Kalaa. The boys have it tough on the streets too. For girls, it is virtually impossible to be on the street and not get picked up by the touts and Madams of the red-light area." Fascinated and full of admiration for the work Neil was doing, his last statement chilled Maya and she breathed a silent prayer thanking the Almighty for saving her Urja.

"You are doing great work. Are you trained in social work? What about others from your family. Are they involved in this work too?" Maya asked spontaneously, full of admiration for Neil's dedication. Maya almost failed to notice the dark cloud that seemed to momentarily pass over Neil's determined and cheerful face.

"This is my family Ma'am," he said, with a sweeping gesture seeming to encompass all the children now gathering up the painting paraphernalia.

"And now I'm afraid you'd need to excuse me. The children are putting up a Bollywood dance number to entertain the conference delegates at the bonfire tonight. I need to see that the music they wanted is in place." Maya bit her lip, wanting to apologise for intruding into what she now realized, was a very private subject. But before she could say anything else, Neil had walked away without a backward glance.

"*Bhaiyya* is great and always has time for everyone. But if he has to talk about his family... He doesn't mean to be rude but feels very sad," Maya turned to look at a stocky, dark figure with thick curly hair, addressing her.

"Oh! I'm sorry, but who are you?" murmured Maya, still wishing she had not asked about Neil's personal life.

"*Didi* (elder sister), I am Shreepati. The younger boys don't know and they never dare to ask Bhaiyya. But I have been with Bhaiyya for 5 years now," he grinned, displaying gleaming buckteeth and a chipped one in front for good measure.

"I used to polish shoes for a living and make Rangolis festive patterns on the pavement in the evenings. Most passersby would rush past, but some would stop and drop a few coins for me, or at least, stop, look and smile. I would often see Bhaiyya arrive in a big chauffeur driven car and enter the Beer Bar, emerging late into the night. He would come in sad and was even sadder when he left, but would quietly hail a taxi and leave. One night, Bhaiyya came out of the Beer Bar even later than usual. His expensive shirt was soiled; the silk tie askew and he barely seemed able to walk. He had been crying and seemed to be mumbling something about not wanting to be without Chubby and Tubby, at least tonight. Before I knew it, he was sick all over my Rangoli on the pavement and had passed out," said Shreepati, screwing up his face at the memory and suddenly ashamed at his impudence in blabbering on about his beloved Bhaiyya to this nice but unknown lady.

Fascinated by the story, Maya encouraged him to go on, promising him she wouldn't repeat the tale to others at the workshop. "Not that anyone would care," she thought wryly, realizing that the cakes of make-up and finery donning process for the bon-fire evening must be in progress in the rooms upstairs. More photo opportunities!

Shreepati continued his tale, describing how it was morning when Bhaiyya came to and was impressed that though Shreepati had been with him all night and even brought him tea from the roadside stall, all the contents of Bhaiyya's pocket were intact. Bhaiyya had told Shreepati about the tragic death of his wife and twin boys in a plane crash exactly a year ago. The whole family was to be on that flight and at the last moment, Neil had had to cancel his plans because of an emergency at work. He blamed himself for their death and hated himself for being alive because of what he had once been obsessed with – but now seemed to do mechanically – work as an investment banker in the 32 storey glass building four streets away.

And then, Bhaiyya had heard Shreepati's story and that of his friends – Chhotu who painted signboards but would rather sketch in charcoal, Bhimraj who painted Ganpati idols during the festival and smuggled away bottles of oil paint... The unusual friendship flourished, the dormant artist in Neil nudged the investment banker to stop sponsoring the Beer Bar's existence and Kalaa was born.

Close to tears for yet another time that evening, Maya gave Shreepati a spontaneous hug. He smiled back shyly. It was dark already. Unconscious that she was still in her day clothes while the others were now turned out in resplendent evening wear, she sat down to enjoy the bonfire evening.

All seemed to be going great with the weekend till the next morning. One of the lady artists emerged from her bedroom, tightly clutching her dressing gown, shrieking, "There's no water in the bathroom!" She had her hair up in tight curlers and her hurriedly wiped face had tell-tale signs of a creamy green substance in the furrows of her forehead.

"Anti-aging screen or some face pack" thought Maya as she watched the pandemonium. Other figures in various stages of the process of dressing emerged from their bedrooms, tempers were running high and the staff at the guest house was in a flurry. The manager mopped his brow as he made yet another futile attempt to explain the situation calmly.

"There has been no electricity for 24 hours, the generator and the inverter have both given up now having kept the show going for the past 12 hours. No water has been pumped up and there is nothing that can be done till the power is back. Getting a water tanker would not be of any use as there is no electricity to pump it all up. Meanwhile, we have informed the bus driver to get here soon, so that he can take people across to another hotel about a half-hour drive from here. Thankfully, that hotel does have power and they have agreed to make some arrangements so that everyone can use their vacant rooms to freshen up." The announcement was met with expressions of irritation, anger, head shaking, tongue-clicking and various other standard modes of disapproval.

"This is the state of a modern town driving distance from the country's political capital. This is what we have come to, decades after independence," sighed a well known artist, his white beard bobbing up and down. The lady with the curlers in her hair was shouting,

"The electricity bit is not in your control. But surely getting us out of here is! At least get this bus around quickly!" Her head was now covered in a silk scarf and she seemed to have her post-shower gear in a chic overnight bag, obviously rearing to go. Maya was reasonably certain the cause of hurry had something to do with the creams and lotions with the curlers and how long those chemicals should be in one's hair before being washed away. But it was not to be. Decibel levels of protest gathered momentum when news filtered in that the bus had a flat tire and could be expected in another hour!

Meanwhile, the children seemed quite unperturbed by the absence of water. In fact, Neil confided that some of the naughty little ones were quite happy to go without the daily showers Neil insisted on! The atmosphere in the porch was heated as the party of adults fretted, fumed, bemoaned the state of the country's infrastructure, snapped at the organizers and one even insisted that they should head for Chandigarh airport and be air-lifted to Delhi immediately.

Suddenly, there was a splash. His eyes and ears alert to ensure the safety of his wards, Neil leapt up and was at the pond within seconds, peeling off his T-shirt to jump in and rescue whoever had accidently fallen into the water. Maya and the others rushed after him, concerned. But Neil was grinning broadly. There in the pond was the naughtiest pair in the bunch of boys, splashing about in glee. Another splash and another... and soon the pond was dotted with delighted brown faces!

"*Bhaiyya log, didi log* (Brothers and sisters), come on in!" shouted one of them, the others joining in the clamour. Reassured that his wards were all confident swimmers, used to splashing about in the polluted Mumbai sea, Neil plunged into the water without a backward glance.

"What's severe inconvenience for some is opportunity for others!" thought Maya.

With his thick black hair plastered to his forehead, Neil was smiling at her expectantly.

"*Chalo didi, jo dar gaya, so mar gaya*" (Come on Sister, be brave. The one who hesitates, is the one who can slip and die!) shouted the impudent Chhotu, spouting staple Bollywood infused dramatic dialogues.

With just a moment's hesitation, Maya rolled up her jeans to her knees and jumped into the water. The artists and sponsors looked appalled. The pond was not exactly a chlorinated swimming pool lined with gleaming blue tiles.

Maya

And clicking pictures with the street children for next year's brochures was fine, but this! Had the erstwhile socialite Mrs. Sikand lost it?

With a twinkle in her eye, Mrs. Mitra gave Maya a knowing smile and ushered the rest away…

33

EPILOGUE

Maya stood on the railway platform at Chandigarh, her feet in sandals braving the nip in the air. She had forgotten her socks, lost in the absent minded behaviour that a gush of new experiences and severe lack of sleep could bring! The last few days had been a dream. After the relatively sanitized and demure conversations at airport lounges she was used to, there was just so much more noise at the railway platform. Of course with entire families turned out to see off an individual on the luxury train to Delhi, there were so many more people. And they had so much more to say to each other.

The wooden beams high up above the train platform seemed to house a congregation of mynah birds. Their collective chirping peaked to an all time high like excited classmates at a wedding of the first of the school friends to get married. Maya looked up at the mynah birds and asked?

"Why are all of you so happy?" She did not expect an answer. The mynah birds had no time to notice anyone who had to think of a reason to be happy. The luxury train chugged on to the platform. Settling into the cosy compartment, she drew the curtains aside. The orange glow of the sun seemed to have burst onto the horizon; impatient to leave the darkness it was submerged in... eager to experience the resplendent glory of the day.

This time Maya did not ask why the sun was so happy.

Author's Profile

Manjiri Gokhale Joshi
Founder Director
Maya CARE Foundation & Elephant Connect Pvt. Ltd.

Since 2009, Manjiri has been running a charity Maya CARE, offering free assistance to senior citizens in India (www.mayacare.com).

A training and management specialist based in the UK, Manjiri has a Master's degree in Mega-Project Management from Said Business School, University of Oxford. She and her husband Abhay Joshi founded Elephant Connect assisting businesses, charities, governments and students achieve their goals through training, project consultancy and tutoring. Manjiri was one of 12 professional experts selected among 13,000 applicants by LinkedIn and Virgin Media to judge, train and mentor entrepreneurs pitching for a £ 1 million fund from Sir Richard Branson. She is a recipient of the British High Commission Chevening scholarship (2006).

She has authored 3 other books:

Inspired-Lessons from 23 contemporary inspirational leaders (co-author Dr. Ganesh Natarajan), Westland 2006;

Crushes, Careers and Cell phones, Foreword- former Miss Universe Sushmita Sen, Vitasta 2011;

Bosses of the wild, Lessons from the corporate jungle, Foreword- Mr. K. V. Kamath, Chairman, ICICI Bank, McGraw Hill 2013.

Among her past assignments are:

Learning & Development Specialist and Head-Project Management (Primal) at Informa PLC, London, Programme Manager- GlobalLogic, UK, National Manager, ICICI Lombard, Mumbai, Head-Contact Centre and Head-Human Resources, Zensar BPO, Assistant Editor-Dataquest, New Delhi and Sub-editor/Reporter, The Indian Express.